# Rants
# Raves
# &
# Ricochets

Stephen Jay Goldberg
2021

ISBN: 978-1-953236-59-3
Library of Congress Control Number: 2021950422

Proof reading: Inger Dybfest
Cover and interior design: Warren Clark

Fomite
58 Peru Street
Burlington, VT 05401
www.fomitepress.com

6-6-2022

# DEDICATION

I **dedicate** this book
to my dear brother
**Jay Goldberg**
1929–1966.

My inspiring love
and wife
**Rachel Bissex**
1956–2005.

GRATITUDES


**Inger Dybfest**
who without which this book
could never have been completed.

**House Wreckers and Mind Fuckers**
from the streets of New York,

The wonderful
**Jazz Musicians**
I've had the joy of playing with and hanging with.

My publisher
**Fomite Press.**

My friend and book designer
**Warren Clark.**

# Contents

# As a child I had this dream:

I was walking in the bright sunlight
by the Atlantic Ocean.

An armadillo appeared out of the sea.

I thought to myself, this can't be real,
I must be dreaming,

I woke up, two men in dark suits were coming up the stairs to my
bedroom carrying a coffin, one in front, one in back.

## I knew the coffin was for me.

Again I thought to myself, this can't be real,
I must be dreaming.

I woke again in my bed,
not sure if I was still dreaming.
Was I awake?

I was nine years old.

## This was over sixty years ago.

The dream comes back so very clearly.

Till this day I have never known

## if I am awake or dreaming.

About to **wake** up.

# IT'S THE NEXT THING

7/18/2011

it's always the next thing
iPod, iPad, iPhone, wifi,
flat screen 3D HD web connected tv

AND THE HAWK STILL FLIES
THE FRIGATES STILL GLIDE
THE WHALES STILL DIVE
SHARKS CLEAR THE WAY

wire recorders, wax recording, stereo
45's, long playing records, CD's, MP3's
rock throwing, catapults, sword fighting, knife fighting
the gun, the hand grenade, automatic killing machine
a-bomb, the h-bomb

THE SPIDER STILL CRAWLS
THE BIRD STILL SINGS
THE LEAVES STILL FALL
THE SUN STILL GLOWS
THE WEEDS STILL GROW

the horse, the horse-drawn carriage
the automobile, the bi-winged airplane
the jet, the space shuttle, the man on the moon
the Hubble telescope

the giant turtles lay their eggs
men steal them to up their virility
viagra, valium, morphine, cocaine
pot, alcohol, heroin, crack, crank it up

rap, hip-hop, DJ's, the beat machines
the click tracks, the synthesizers
the vibrators, the online porn
the Netflix, the no-flicks

so where the fuck is Bach
where is Beethoven
where is Mahler
where is Shakespeare

4 track recorders
a million track digital recorders
where is Charlie Parker
where is Miles Davis
where is anything

AND THE HAWK STILL FLIES
THE FRIGATES STILL GLIDE
THE WHALES STILL DIVE
SHARKS CLEAR THE WAY

and where is the babe
you always wanted
where is the lover
you never had

and yeah death
will it be slow, painful and alone
or in an expensive nursing home
when you don't get who
the fuck anybody is
staring at a flat screen tv
stoned on morphine

then **bam**
it's at last over
**bam, bam, bam**
three last heartbeats
in 3/4 time
like the lost drum machine
you never had

no more thinking
no more getting better
no more what you missed
no more books you didn't read
or lovers you didn't have

it's just simple black
easy, nothing
we all look good in black

AND THE BIRDS FLY AND SING
THE WHALES DIVE
THE WEEDS GROW

men mow their lawns
as if it had meaning
make life better
to cut the fucking grass
and they too go to no place
after kissing the children goodnight

I've known such heroes
who have never touched
a lawn mower
pulled that idiot unforgivable
starter cord that never works

tiny baby turtles walk into
the huge breaking pacific waves
not many will survive
that's the deal, how the song goes

# BIRDS FLY, FISH SWIM
## I DRINK

# DAD'S DARKROOM

## *My* dad

*My* dad was really into photography, he had one of those box cameras you look down into. In a small room behind the bar was his darkroom. The bar had his initials on the front in large wooden letters JAG, Joseph Arthur Goldberg. His darkroom contained an enlarger, trays for the chemicals, lit by a soft orange bulb. Sometimes he'd let me come in with him and watch the 8x10's slowly appear magically in the developer tray, then into the stop bath, then the water. I don't remember him explaining much of it to me, but it was nice being in there with him, with the smell of the chemicals and his cigar smoke. He would do many renderings of the same photo till he felt it was just right. I must have been sitting on a bar stool so I could see what he was doing.

On the knotty pine basement wall there were framed photographs of the women of the "Ethical Culture Group," all in their bras and underwear, my mother with a big cigarette holder, looking very elegant. I liked it, dad must have had much fun taking them.

My father was a furrier, Goldberg Schaffer Furs, they manufactured and sold women's fur coats, Mink and Persian Lamb. "The Place" as it was called was on Seventh Avenue in Manhattan in the fur district. I remember going there and sweeping the floors and getting a dollar. I was the only kid that had mink tails on his bike handles.

When it fell apart for him, he lost his business, gone. Mom, years later, told me she never knew anything about their finances. Dad would just ask, is there anything you want or need? And she would have it.

Then the house was sold, we moved into a small apartment on Dartmouth Street, still in Forest Hills. Dad was never the same. Lost their group of friends because they could no longer afford the Copa, trips to Miami and the Catskills.

## No darkroom.

Me as a kid starting high school did not understand. But worse, did not show any compassion for his loss. He, dad, would walk around that apartment like a caged animal. I know that's what killed him at 57, the idea of failure, to not provide for his family the way he had been. It wasn't the leukemia, it was the loss of pride when money meant much.

As a child he would take me in the stall shower with him and shampoo my hair, he seemed so big to me, me so small. He liked to show me this photo of himself the summer he had worked as a lumberjack. He was really so handsome, he looked like Clark Gable.

He liked to tell me that after the lumberjack summer, his arms wouldn't fit through the clothes he had worn there because he had gotten so muscular. We both enjoyed the story, I wish I had that photograph of him.

The smell of his cigar smoke, the Sunday mornings I would come into his bed and he'd read me the funny papers. Make some "puts", which were farts, and laugh, he was a great dad until I became an arrogant teenager, trying to be cool while he was losing everything.

After we moved, he'd bring home "skins," fur pieces. He'd put a 4x8 piece of plywood on the dinning room table and proceed to staple them down, in order to fit them together like a jigsaw puzzle, then to be sewn together to make a fur coat. It was complicated, highly skilled work.

No more big place with women on sewing machines, many tables with skins being arranged, a complex security system and a vault to keep the expensive fur coats in. No more nice house to come home to, no more stall shower, no more darkroom to watch the black and white images magically appear in the developer tray.

## No more developer tray. No more.

# Frank Dupree

TONIGHT IN CALIFORNIA
LOOKING AT A CRESCENT MOON
LISTENING TO CHET BAKER
SO TENDER
ALL OF IT

I THINK OF OLD FRIEND
FRANK DUPREE

FRANK PLAYED TENOR SAXOPHONE
HE WORKED AS A LONGSHOREMAN
HE WAS A BODY BUILDER
MISSING SOME TEETH
FROM ALCOHOL, CIGARETTES
AND SADNESS

ON CLINTON STREET
THE LOWER EAST SIDE OF NEW YORK

HE HAD A TATTOO
THE NAME OF A LOST LOVE
ON HIS ARM

HE HAD A TINY APARTMENT
ON THE GROUND FLOOR
CLINTON STREET
AND A GIRLFRIEND
NOT THE ONE ON HIS ARM

ONE NIGHT WHEN HE WAS DRUNK
AND SHE WAS SLEEPING
HE CUT OFF HER HAIR

SHE HAD NICE BREASTS
I KNOW THAT BECAUSE
ONE NIGHT WHEN FRANK
WASN'T HOME
I ASKED IF I COULD SKETCH HER
NUDE
NICE BREASTS

I THINK OF FRANK TONIGHT
BECAUSE OF THE MOON

ONE SUMMER NIGHT
WE WENT UP ON THE ROOF
OF THE PLACE ON STANTON STREET
OFF CLINTON
FRANK WITH HIS TENOR AND BEER
ME WITH MY TRUMPET
AND CHEAP WINE
OR MAYBE IT WAS ALL CHEAP WINE

MAX WAS PLAYING BRUSHES
THE MOON WAS FULL
WE PLAYED
HOW HIGH THE MOON
THOUSANDS OF CHORUSES

I WAS IN MY TWENTIES
IT WAS ALL SO BEAUTIFUL
IT DIDN'T MATTER HOW GOOD IT WAS
WE WERE PLAYING FOR THE MOON

WE PASSED OUT
ONE BY ONE
I WOKE IN THE HOT TAR
IN THE BLASTING SUN

## Everyone gone

FRANK WAS TOLD HIS LIVER WAS GONE
SO HE SWITCHED TO HEROIN
FOR HIS HEALTH
HIS PLACE BECAME A SHOOTING GALLERY
IN EXCHANGE FOR DOPE

I WONDER IF HE EVER
PUT THE NEEDLE IN THE LOST LOVE TATTOO
I WOULD HAVE
I'M SURE HE DID
FRANK WAS A ROMANTIC

I HADN'T SEEN FRANK FOR A YEAR OR SO
I MET HIM IN WASHINGTON SQUARE
HE LOOKED SO STONED
EYES LIKE GLASS
THAT MOMENT IS LIKE A PHOTOGRAPH
LOOKING INTO FRANK'S EYES

FRANK WAS FOUND DEAD
IN HIS LITTLE SHOOTING GALLERY
NOT BY FRIENDS OR LOVERS
BUT BY THE STINK OF HIS ROTTING CORPSE

# how high
# the moon

STEPHEN JAY GOLDBERG

**10**

# A Leather Tongue 2/26/87

a leather tongue
hangs
near the unused thoughts

refrigerator filled
with
unopened frozen mail

pages from a book of jokes
stare at each other

uncared for
food
rots on white formica

a flying thing leaves a jet trail
dangerously close to the stained ceiling

the balloon heads below
that continually repeat
the same conversation
about the same works of art
with the same intonation
that reinforces rightness

milk spills on the table
runs down the legs
to the floor
making a series of white lakes and winding white rivers
containing neither fish nor plant
nor recreational crafts pulling
grinning water skiers

a slick touched up photograph
of a cult worshipped movie star's head
behind glass on a wall
adding the insult of style

as if concept weren't enough

# Booze

I don't mean to write so much about booze, but it has been a huge part of my life, good and bad, bad and good. It has saved me many times and yes destroyed much. I put more on the plus side. It often supplied the guts I didn't have, gave me comfort when nothing else did, stimulated creativity. As they say, got me out of my own way.

The human brain is a very strange piece of meat, how it likes to defeat itself. How this very strong and legal, this not so innocent chemical, can affect it. Of course I can only speak for myself. No, I won't go into a drunk-o-log. This happened and that happened stuff, and much has happened and almost happened and did not happen.

At first everything feels better, easy, independent and strong. Then coordination starts to go, in the wrists and legs. Thoughts become random, connected yet unconnected like the movement of clouds in the sky. Feeling so not alone, like a friend or lover is inside you. Then you want more of that beautiful feeling, so you pour another drink, to make that internal feeling even better and better. Yes it does work, it does get better and even more beautiful and less lonely. The lover/friend is inside your body, your blood, your heart. There is a moment of feeling really thankful that you have this dear internal friend.

And yes, you treat it well, nice glass, fresh ice, good mixture. Respect for the bottle. As you would treat a friend.

Then comes the no function part, sort of funny and it brings a smile. Time for the horror sleep. Try to make it up the stairs. Hold on to the railings, proud to make it up the stairs, knowing a sleep might come. No bed spinning or throwing up, I am a pro at this. No pissing in the bed, except a few times a year, no big deal. Put something under the sheets and mattress cover and put a fan on top, it dries the piss right up, no smell or anything. Booze piss has no scent and not much color.

I have been neglecting stuff, putting stuff off, these pain pills during the day the booze at night. In pain, harder to walk and breathe. Sort of a very slow drowning. At this point better to die from booze than from cancer. Dying from booze is my choice, dying from cancer is cancer's choice. We humans like to have the illusion that we are in charge of our own destiny. A grand illusion. Cancer eats me, I drink the drink. My choice. This ant life goes no matter what!

Oh yeah, the heroes. I remember seeing Tennessee Williams on a late night talk show, really stoned, then he told Johnny how he had stopped drinking. Mom had a poster on her wall of Dean Martin smiling with a drink in his hand. I would see Norman Mailer come into the all night dinner on 6th avenue, Greenwich Village, with interesting women, pretty loaded. Bukowski loved the booze. Jack London wrote, "I fell into the river so very drunk, almost drowned. Imagine how bad it must be for those poor alcoholics." Writing is so isolating.

The jazz greats more into heroin, almost all of them. You can't play when you are really drunk. It feels like you can. I guess you can on heroin. No, I never tried it. I saw too many good people die from it when I was young.

**14**

Does the booze or drugs make a genius? No, of course not. Do I think I am a genius? Embarrassing question. Of course I do. Mostly when I drink! I feel inspired, on fire, full of power, confident, can do no wrong, not lazy, sexy, so brilliantly creative. It really does work like that for me. If it is an illusion I'll take it. It gets stuff done.

In the morning, when I read stuff back, or listen to recordings that I have made last night, some of it, not all of it, really good, some not so good. If I had no drinks I would have sat in front of the TV, eating crap I didn't want to eat. Then shutting off the TV, feeling really bad about the wasted night. Up to the lonely, empty bed unable to sleep. Listening to the boring npr brit radio, feeling so terribly alone.

Missing my dead/love wife. Missing my life of performing as a jazz musician, missing directing the many plays I have written, missing being young and playing tennis and sailing and making love under sail, missing being really handsome, missing not knowing the future, missing walking without pain, missing incredible strength I had.

So now the medication of choice is booze. I would like to find a better one, like cocaine mixed with booze, cocaine the energy, booze the freedom. Then buy hookers, for an old man sex is the life force, real pros who know what they are doing, certainly worth the money. Pay her and she goes away. Nice fair deal.

No more love left, a fair deal. I've had my love. Death, not a bad deal.

# J**ay** my ░big░
## brother

**Jay was the most important figure in my life, he died at thirty-seven from cancer, I'll go into that later. Why I'm still alive I don't know.**

I remember the day he got his draft notice, we were in our bedroom when he showed it to me. It began, **"Greetings,"** then he showed me the famous nude photo of Marilyn Monroe. It was the Korean War. Before he left, he told me, **"Don't listen to mom and dad they don't know a fuckin' thing."**

I had this plastic toy instrument with holes to make different notes. I went into Jay's saxophone case, took out the mouthpiece, shaved it down with a knife so it would fit on this plastic thing, was he pissed off, mom and dad bought him a new one, I had to do chores to pay for it. I don't think it ever did work. I remember one night Jay coming home late, **I woke to the sound of him throwing up**, I yelled out, **"Mommy Jay's sick!"** Of course he was drunk, they, dad, dragged him out of bed and put him in a cold shower, **I heard him yelling and laughing at the same time.**

We had a summer bungalow in Long Beach, Long Island, I loved that place. 90 Nebraska Street. One afternoon Jay made this cooler of what he called **"Purple Jesus,"** grape juice and gin. We had straws and drank it right from the cooler on the beach, maybe my first drunk, I loved it too. This was before Korea.

I loved Jay so much, still do, my real guru.

# SAYULITA MEXICO

after rachel died 2/20/05
I knew I couldn't face another
vermont winter in our house
alone

a friend told me
there's a little town
in mexico you would like
sayulita

better than the house
and the freezing dark winter
i didn't know a soul there
so I somehow
got on a plane and went

I had taken spanish
in high school
failed a few times
didn't realize anything

getting off the plane at night
in puerto valliarta
not remembering it was the place
where the film night of the iguana
was made

somehow finding the bus
the driver said something to me
a woman said two pesos
she paid it for me

I was truly lost
in another world
at least I knew why
I was alone

wandering the town
finding the cheapest hotel
stranger in a strange land
the warm dark wind feeling okay

thinking I remember
leaving from my son's
house in new jersey
he said dad
why is your bag so heavy
there were four half gallons
of vodka in it
he said
dad
they might have
vodka in mexico

they did

sometimes
in blindness and desperation
we make good choices
it was one of them

# Corpse

4/23/86

corpse
on a flat expanse of white stone

huge birds
pick
with
elongated razor beaks
at
the emaciated body
leaving
only the nervous system
perfectly intact on the skeleton

hot sun
heats the nerve strands
taut across the bones
a wind blows
the nerves vibrate
an ever ascending harmonically complex music
shoots skyward

one by one
the strands burst
leaving
delicate popping sounds
each a different pitch

the skeleton
left
to cast shadow and line
for centuries
on the soundless white stone

s goldberg

# O m a r

**My grandmother,** mother's mother, lived with us, I called her Omar, she was a widow, her husband died in Europe. We had three bedrooms, Omar shared a bedroom with me. I remember as a child falling asleep holding her hand, reciting a prayer together in Yiddish. She was so very kind to me.

**One day** there was just an empty, neatly made bed. Where was Omar? I had no idea. The introduction of alone. I couldn't remember the prayer without the unison of our voices. Just an innocent child with no idea of past or future. I can still feel that child inside me, right in my center. Surrounded by need.

**Omar died** when I was four or five, I just remember the empty made bed next to mine, no hand to hold, she was there, then she wasn't. I think it was then that mother decided she could discipline me the way I should be disciplined.

## That's when the trouble started and everything changed.

Rants Raves & Ricochets

**19**

# Montreal 8/13/03

the night is long
always afraid of the dark
to be alone in the darkness
In the horror bed alone

**the year in Montreal
was something**

I was alone
Holly was in Paris
me in New York
East Ninth Street
between 5th Avenue and University Place

the tv on
**Bobby Kennedy got shot
on live tv**
it seemed like 2 AM

I got dressed and went to
Max's Kansas City
the hip New York
Andy Warhol hangout bar

I met a tall woman
model woman
in an antique velvet dress

I told her I was leaving
this USA in the morning
she said
in a beautiful accent
I go with you

the next day we're on a plane
she with a straw basket
with all her belongings
out of the Warhol crowd
away from her lesbian lover

we found a place to stay
she read me Winnie the Pooh
which sounded like vinnie the pooh
a gangster book
we planned to go to Newfoundland
it just sounded good
new-found-land

maybe she was a famous model
it didn't matter
we were having fun
she decorated the room
with her beautiful clothes

the interesting thing was
she frightened men
because she was so beautiful
and eccentric

rose in her teeth
so tall
beautiful clothes
I loved that she
terrified men

we'd walk the streets of Montreal
she made me feel like a movie star

she was so kind to me
soft, a star
I can't remember her name

I sat in at a jazz club
the Black Bottom
the music was great
made a friend Brian Barley
a great saxophone player

he invited us to live with him
he had an extra room
just off Saint Catherine street

**we made a band
a great band
and became like brothers
the best players in Montreal**

I slept with her every night
in that little room
she would read me to sleep
no matter how drunk I was

until I brought another woman home
a woman from England
I remember her name
Sally Scott, a hot redhead
with a good sense of humor

then the beautiful woman was gone

then I fucked it all up
the woman invited me to England
she told me she was rich
had horses and stables

I didn't go

I lost all the gigs
had no place to live
knocked on a door
Montreal was getting cold

there she was
me exhausted, trumpet
under the arm
she let me stay with her
read me to sleep

the sheets were so clean
warm and safe

Montreal

I don't remember her name
the model with the accent
who had slept in
Salvador Dali's garden

I stay afraid of the dark
afraid to sleep alone

# S A U L **STOLLMAN**

**I** met Saul through his younger brother Norman, who I went to high school with. I was living in New York City in my twenties and needed a job, needed money. I knew Saul was an industrial designer. He made things and I was good with my hands, good at making things.

I called him and went up to his loft on 22nd street where he lived. We talked and he gave me a job. He said come in tomorrow at 10. When I got there, on time, he was still in bed. I liked him right off. He had a wonderful state of the art stereo system, classical music always playing. Saul had all kinds of tools, drill press, sander, table saw and much more. He also had many impressive paintings that he had done, hanging on his walls.

The Stollmans had this very different speech pattern, not Brit but articulate, fast and clear, they sounded smart.

Saul paid me minimum wage which at that time was $1.50 an hour, which was fine with me. What was nice was there were always different projects. I remember us doing a store interior out on Long Island, we'd go out there at 10 or 11pm and work through the night. I think Saul had a VW bug. Always interesting conversation, this was the 60's.

Saul seemed to be a loner, I never saw him with any friends or women, yet I felt like we were friends, good friends.

Sometimes we'd be working on a project in his loft and we couldn't find a certain needed tool. He didn't want to waste time looking for it so he'd send me down to the hardware store to buy a new one, even though he might have three of them.

One time I was having a hard time with my then young wife, I was 21, she was 17. We were homeless so Saul let us stay with him. I guess while I was out he had done a nude painting of her. I saw the painting and never asked, it was her. I didn't mind, it was a good piece of art. That marriage never worked out.

Another time, I met Saul at McDonalds on West 3rd Street. He was sitting in front of two Big Macs, he had clipped a coupon, he said, "Why do I want two of something I don't want one of." I thought that was so brilliant and funny, still do.

Right after Bobby Kennedy got shot I so much wanted to go to Montreal, I asked Saul to lend me a hundred bucks. He did and said, you better pay me back, which I did. It was a life changing trip for me and my music.

Now this is a very strange story about Saul, it sort of defines his loneliness. I hope he wouldn't mind me sharing it.

He had gotten a phone call from a woman about doing some sort of work. Then more phone calls with this woman and more phone calls. When I tried to call Saul his phone was always busy, I mean always. The calls seemed to go on day and night. At one point Saul had to get another phone line. This went on for weeks, months. And yes he told me all about it.

Then she told him her photo was on a certain page of the current issue of Vogue magazine, a lingerie ad. She said it embarrassed her and would he buy up all the mags. So crazy that he bought many of them. Imagine, he told me all this stuff. I did tell him it was nuts, but it went on. Finally she gave him an address in the Bronx and he went. The door opened a crack and a voice and eyes said, she's not in. Such a sad story about such an intelligent man.

Saul was always a good friend to me and I hope me to him. Much respect and love.

The last time we spoke, he said, "I can't walk," as if to say how ridiculous is that.

I could write and write about Saul Stollman, a truly one of a kind interesting man. Glad to have had him as a friend.

S.G.

# White Ashes

I don't know where you are
I know you're not
in the white ashes
they delivered
that horrible confusing morning

I remember saying to the guy
who took your body away

## make sure you bring
## me the right ashes

he said
we have only one cremation today
so there won't be any chance of mistake
it seemed to matter to me
not to get the wrong ashes

I admit
I do try to imagine
you in that fire
I remember saying
please be gentle

how can a fire
burning a human body
be gentle
I just meant the way they handled you
in your nightgown
death gown

deep down
I didn't want them to
remove the nightgown
or put you in some bag

knowing you were
no longer in that
pained medicated
beautiful body
you were truly gone forever

the only word that came to mind
was impossible
way past the breaking
waves of confusion

something a brain can't process
my brain can't process
not having you here
with your smile and love and music
and yes body

memories are a beautiful hell
that was given to me
to try to live with
and you left us so much

## i wanted so badly
## to climb into that cremation fire with you

to hold you as we burned together
but our daughter held my hand
and said
please dad don't

it was the tone and the word "dad" that got me
to not leave our child an orphan
to not burn up with you
so baby I go on without you
worse than losing a limb
my worst horror

we would joke
because I was
so much older than you

I would say
after I die
knowing I would die first
almost twenty years older
please baby don't fuck
anyone for at least a week after I die

you would joke and say
a week
that's a long time

all the men and women
loved you
so beautiful and sexy
natural in your way
of being
your scent
and your soul

we were through so much
you and I

then the cancer
came in
the devil
that would destroy everything
no holding it back
no matter what we tried

radiation
chemo
morphine
hospice

you the good one
the beauty
the kindness
the mother

and now in this moment
the morning light
coming through the windows
of our house

## I avoid going up to our bed
## ashtray filled

glass of vodka in hand
I avoid sleeping in the room you
died in and suffered in
the room we made perfect love in

birds singing
or is it crying
or begging
light getting brighter
feet so cold

it's all so very fragile
I miss you sweet baby
I miss you
in this silence

the birds have stopped singing

I admit
I went through your drawers
and closet
just to find something
that had your scent

there was nothing

I can't wait to be
with you
in no-place

## but I will wait
## just a bit

# FOX HOLE

c1993 Stephen Goldberg

THIS SENSE OF ALWAYS FALLING
THROUGH THE SAND
THROUGH THE CEMENT
FROM THE BEGINNING TILL NOW
IT NEVER STOPS

WHO IS IT THAT FINDS THIS NEED
TO SAY
I AM FALLING
I AM A LIVING FALLING THING

THE CONFESSION HERE
IN THIS LARGE CELL

THE BARS FIRST STRAIGHT
THEN THE SLOW CURVE OF TIME
THE MINUTE CHANGES IN TEMPERATURE
THAT I HAD BEGUN TO CRAVE
HYDRATION THEN DEHYDRATION

THE GAP OF IMAGINATION
THE LOOSENING OF THE
BOLTS OF SANITY

TEMPERATURES CHILL THEN BOIL
THE ALTERNATING CURRENT OF CHANGE

WIRES ARE HUNG BETWEEN THE BARS
THE BARS SO CLOSE TOGETHER
OR IS IT FAR APART
TELLING EACH OTHER IN SOME WIRE LANGUAGE
HOW TO STAND
HOW TO CURVE
AND WHERE OR WHEN TO SPIRAL
AT WHAT TEMPO TO SPIN

IS SHE TALKING TO ME?

NO I DON'T THINK SO
ARE THE BARS SO CLOSE TOGETHER
OR IS THE DISTANCE TO THEM SO GREAT
THAT THEY APPEAR TO BE SOLID
WHO KNOWS WHO CAN TELL

THE POLLUTION OF SPECULATION
MAKES IT HARD TO BREATHE
SO THE NOSTRILS ENLARGE
AND THE LUNGS GROW SPARES
EVER ADJUSTING TO A HOSTILE ENVIRONMENT
YET ALWAYS A LITTLE BEHIND
A LITTLE TOO SLOW FOR IT EVER
TO BE PAINLESS

IS THAT HER TALKING TO ME?
NO HER EYES AND WORDS
PASS OVER ME AS IF I WEREN'T HERE
AS IF I WASN'T WORTH JUDGING
AS IF I WEREN'T WORTH BEING TOLD
WHAT TO DO OR WHEN TO MOVE
AND WHAT NOT TO TOUCH BECAUSE OF
TEMPERATURE OR SHARPNESS

"DON'T FALL ON THE BROKEN BOTTLE OR SHARPENED SPEAR"
HOW I WISH SHE COULD HAVE SAID IT TO ME
LOOKING DIRECTLY AT ME
NOT BACKGROUND OR FOREGROUND
DIRECTLY AT ME
AND SAID IT IN THAT VOICE OF HERS
"DON'T FALL ON THE BROKEN BOTTLE OR SHARPENED SPEAR"
NO I NEVER WAS WORTH IT

THE TIME LONG PASSED
NOT THAT IT WOULD HAVE MATTERED
OR THAT I WOULD HAVE LISTENED
THE TIME HAS SINCE PASSED

THE SYNCHRONIZATION OF THE SLIDING NOW
AND THE SLIPPERY PAST
THE THEN HAS ALWAYS HAD
A DEFECTIVE FOCUSING MECHANISM
VERY MUCH LIKE
ALWAYS BEING LIED TO

NOT BEING ABLE TO SEPARATE
WHAT IS INTENTIONAL AND WHAT IS NOT
UNABLE TO SEE THINGS AS THEY ARE

EVERYTHING THEN PUT INTO
A GEOMETRIC PATTERN
ALWAYS MADE TO FIT THE CURRENT THEORY
THE ONE IN STYLE
WHETHER IT BE GERMAN FRENCH OR ITALIAN
THE QUANTIZATION ALWAYS GETTING TIGHTER
AMONGST THE PIXELS

WAS THAT HER SPEAKING TO ME?
NO OF COURSE NOT
WHY SHOULD SHE

I WAS ALWAYS SO WELL BEHAVED
MAKING TINY ADJUSTMENTS
ON MY JANIS-ARABIAN ELECTRONIC KEYBOARD

THE STORIES SHE READ ME
ALWAYS ON TAPE
HER RARELY BEING PHYSICALLY PRESENT
THE STORIES WERE ALWAYS ABOUT SILENCE
I WANTED TO ACCOMPANY THEM ON MY KEYBOARD
BUT THE MORALS
WERE IMPOSSIBLE TO COMBAT

NO ONE SEEMED TO HEAR ME OR SEE ME
IT WASN'T TILL MY TEENS
THAT I REALIZED ABOUT THE GLASS OR PLASTIC
THE CLEAR WALL
THAT HAD ALWAYS BEEN THERE

STEPHEN JAY GOLDBERG

SHE HAD LIPS ALL RIGHT
THE DAY I GOT OUT
RELEASED BY THE TRAGIC LOOKING
UNIFORMED MEN AND WOMEN
I HEARD HER VOICE
HER ACTUAL VOICE
"IT'S OKAY TAKE HIM AWAY"
OR MAYBE SHE SAID
"TAKE IT AWAY"
IT SOUNDED SO KIND AND DECENT
ANCIENT

LIPS ON ICE LIPS ON GLASS

AND GOOD RIDDANCE I THOUGHT
AS I'M SURE SHE DID

WAS THAT HER
SPEAKING TO ME JUST THEN
I SUPPOSE NOT

THE IMPRISONMENT NOW
IS SO MUCH MORE SUBTLE
NO GUARDS
THE BARS EVER CHANGING
SO I AM EVER ADJUSTING TO THE LIMITS I DEFINE

WHETHER I'M OUTSIDE OR IN
COLD OR WARM
DRESSED OR UNDRESSED

I OFTEN FIND MYSELF BRUISED
ON THE FACE THE SHOULDERS
THE BACK THE THIGHS

I HAVE NO MEMORY
OF SUFFERING ANY BEATINGS OR ENCOUNTERS
THEY HEAL QUICKLY
AND WHEN THEY'RE GONE
IT'S AS IF THEY NEVER EXISTED

NO ONE ELSE SEES THEM
BECAUSE THERE IS NO ONE ELSE
NO ONE IN MY ORBIT OF EXISTENCE

I HAVE NOTHING TO COMPARE MY IMPULSES TO
THERE SEEM TO BE
SOME SORT OF PHANTOMS OUT THERE
I AM NOT THE ONLY THING THAT MOVES
AT TIMES I CAN FEEL THEIR BREATH ON MY WOUNDS
AT TIMES I THINK I CAN HEAR THEIR HEARTBEATS
AS I CONCENTRATE ON THE UNEVENNESS OF THE PULSE
IT FADES AND IS GONE

THAT WAS HER SAYING
"BRUSH YOUR HAIR BRUSH YOUR TEETH PUT YOUR THINGS AWAY"
WHAT IS THE DIFFERENCE

I CLIMB THE HILL EVERY DAY
ASCENDING TO ITS FLAT TOP
LIKE AN INVERTED NIPPLE

I CRAWL INTO MY FOXHOLE
REST MY HEAD
AND WATCH THE CLOUDS AND BIRDS GO BY
AND SOON IT HAS TAKEN OVER
MY HEAD SEEMINGLY CONNECTED TO THE GROUND
CONNECTED TO THE EARTH IT RESTS ON
THE POWER SWITCH TURNED ON
HER VOICE SAYS
"TURN IT DOWN YOU'RE GOING TO BURN IT YOU'RE GOING TO RUIN IT
ALL"

SOMETIMES THE VOICE
HER VOICE AND MINE MUTTER DIRECTIONS TOGETHER
AT THE SAME TIME
IN BOTH UNISON AND COUNTERPOINT
MINE ALWAYS TRYING TO FIT WITH HERS
HERS THE STEADY ONE THE DEPENDABLE ONE
IT'S ONLY ENTRANCES AND EXITS I CAN'T PREDICT

OFTEN DAYS AND WEEKS GO BY WITHOUT THE VOICE

34

HER VOICE
THEN AFTER AWHILE
I FORGET IT'S ABSENCE
THEN FROM WITHIN THE SILENCE IT APPEARS
WITH NO CRESCENDO NO BUILD UP
AS IF IT WERE ALWAYS CLOSE AND WAITING
TILL IT WAS FORGOTTEN

NONE OF IT MAKES A DIFFERENCE
REHEARSING ONE'S DISINTEGRATION
PRACTICING MERGING WITH THE SOIL

CEMENT
HARDENED SAND

I AM NOT AWARE OF IT
ALL THE THINGS THAT HAVE NOT
PASSED THROUGH THE PENLIGHT OF MY AWARENESS
THINGS THAT GO ON BEING THERE
ME HAVING NO RECOGNITION OF THEM

I HAVE BEEN CAUGHT IN MY OWN TRAP
THAT WAS SHOVELED WITH THE AID OF NO SHOVEL OR DEVICE

AT FIRST TO BE COOL
IN THE FRESHLY DUG HOLE
BUT IT WAS MORE THAN COMFORT
A COMFORT I HAD NEVER KNOWN

AS IT BECAME DARK
I BECAME FEARFUL OF
SPENDING THE NIGHT UP THERE
IN THE BLACKNESS
I HAD FORGOTTEN THE MOON AND STARS
TILL THIS MOMENT

MY LIFE BEING THE VOICE SAYING
«THAT'S WRONG YOU'RE MISSING OUT»
LIPS ON GLASS LIPS ON ICE

I STOPPED CALCULATING AND TAKING INVENTORY

THE PRISON FOR ME EXPANDED

ON THAT MORNING
ARRIVING AT MY FOX HOLE
AS I SLID IN
TO MY SHOCK
THERE WAS A BODY
ANOTHER PERSON
HOW MY INSTINCT TOLD ME TO RUN
TO HIDE
BUT IT WAS MY HOLE
THAT I HAD DUG
THAT I HAD INVERTED

I SLUNG MY HEAD OVER THE EDGE
AND NO MORE THAN TWO FEET AWAY
SHE LAY
THE FORM MOST ASSUREDLY FEMALE
IT BORE NO SHOULDERS OR BODY HAIR OR PENIS

THE VOICE SAID
"GO TO YOUR ROOM IF YOU CAN'T EAT GO TO YOUR ROOM"

THE SKIN ON THE BODY
THAT LAID THERE
TAKING UP A GOOD PORTION OF THE VERY
FOXHOLE THAT I HAD DUG
THE BODY PALE
RIBS SHOWING
AND BETWEEN CROSSED ARMS THE BREASTS
AND THE SLIGHT BEATING HEARTBEAT
I SLID DOWN NEXT TO IT
THIS WAS THE HOLE I HAD DUG

I THOUGHT
SO HIDDEN SO APART
I COULD FEEL AT MY FINGERTIPS
THE CLAWS I HAD DUG MY HOLE WITH
I TRIED TO SOMEHOW OCCUPY THE HOLE WITH IT

IT JUMPED

I FELT A BRIGHT FLASH IN MY HEAD
WHEN I RECOVERED IT WAS GONE
I WAS THANKFUL THE SKY REMAINED GRAY
BRIGHT SUNLIGHT WOULD HAVE BEEN TOO MUCH TO BEAR

I COULD FEEL THE BRUISE
STILL OPEN ON MY HEAD
THE ORIGIN OF THE BRUISE
HAD BEEN A STONE
A STONE IN A HAND

PARTS OF HER HAD LEFT IMPRESSIONS
IN PARTS OF THE HOLE
AN ELBOW
A KNEE
A FOOT

I PLACED MY ELBOW
IN THE ELBOW IMPRESSION SHE HAD LEFT
MY THROAT TIGHTENED
THE TEARS CAME
I LET THEM DROP INTO THE FOOTPRINT
THEY BECAME LITTLE INVERTED INSECT BITES
ON THE SOLE OF A FOOT THAT INVADED ME

THE VOICE WAS ABSENT
I LAY AGAIN IN MY HOLE
LOOKING UP
INTO THE GRAY SKY

THE VOICE WHISPERED
"DON'T FALL ON THE BROKEN BOTTLE OR SHARPENED SPEARS"

Dear Stephen,

It's that time of year to review your Medicare plan options to ensure your prescription drugs will still be covered in 2021. There may also be changes to your 2021 Medicare plan benefits due to COVID-19. It's important to **make sure you have the plan that can save you the most money**, including copays as low as $0 when you enroll in select plans.*

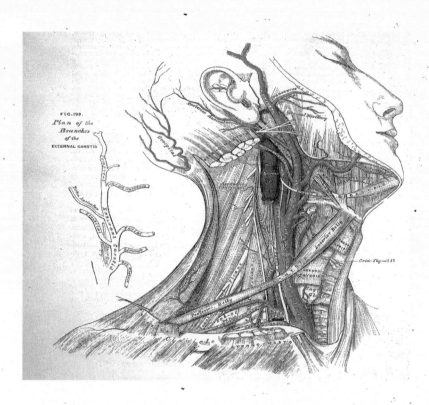

FIG.190. Plan of the Branches of the EXTERNAL CAROTID

I saw this beautiful dead bird on my deck, almost brought to tears and yes wonderment. It was so still. This thing that could fly with freedom, make a nest, reproduce, a way of living I could never understand or imagine, being up there flying in the magical sky. With more freedom that we can ever know. It was so very dead I couldn't touch it.

It made it clear how real death is, a little bird.

# Death

## I have only watched two people die, my brother and my wife.

My brother was 37, my wife was 48. Both from cancer. I am now 81 and miss them both much, they were/are the most important figures in my life. So it's like going off a diving board, if they did it I can do it, will do it and had so much more time living and wasting.

## The strange thing about cancer, when it kills the host it kills itself. Why would something do that?

What is wasting time? Waiting for it to pass till the next thing. Yet time is so abstract. A concert pianist thinking, if I am not practicing I'm wasting time; a junkie, if I'm not out copping I'm wasting time. Not pursuing what is most important is a waste of time. "Yeah you could have been great but you wasted too much time. Now you're on your death bed and it was your mistaken choice."

So easy to be lazy. I'll do it later, I don't care, it makes no difference, I'm really tired. Sleep, the nightly death.

So what the hell are we so afraid of. You say, well it's an every day deal except we breathe and dream and move, heart beating, blood flowing and we awaken.

I think it's something/nature is telling us; this is a hint to what it's like, so don't get too freaked out. It's the same as sleep except you don't wake up, ever. You don't get to make coffee, go to the bathroom, take a shower, read the paper, go to work (if you work), say good morning, watch tv, make love, walk, see the sky, go shopping, make phone calls, eat, breathe, make money, spend money, think.

You don't get to feel pain, cry, age, miss anything, work, feel sad, feel alone, look in the mirror, get sick, take pills, drink, diet, worry, watch your life go by, worry about death like missing the bus, or burning the toast, or eating too many carbs, getting fat and ugly, smoking, being broke, homeless, going to jail, failing, breaking legs, getting cancer, not being loved...so very much to worry about knowing worrying is wasted time, time that can never be gotten back. More to worry about. Wasted time.

At this point I don't worry about all the above things and more. I could if I chose too, another form of entertainment. Makes one feel like a caring person. "I worry about you."

## (hey pretty loaded, feel okay, sleep in bed waiting for me, it's okay)

# aging shit

YEAH IT'S PAINFUL
EVERY PART OF EVERYTHING
IN PAIN
MORE THINGS UNDOABLE
IT STARTS SMALL

> eye glasses
> opening a jar
> standing quickly
> night driving
> name forgetting
> ringing in the ears

THEN SLOWLY BIGGER

> sleep interruptions
> endless night pissing
> balance off
> always tired
> skin hanging
> looking self ugly

THEN

> hard to walk
> can't work the tv remote
> no bladder control
> losing things
> dark depression

the biggest is sex
when that is gone
all is gone
fuck the whole
big deal

i'm still good
but see the future
not so good
the disaster of netflix

A NETFLIX LIFE

better to off oneself
while the wits are available

LAST PHASE

no memory
netflix incomprehensible
friends and family gone
diapers in a stinking home
mistaking a chair for a dog
gone

# All I care about

OCTOBER 2019

it seems all I care about
is playing drunk chess
with people all over the world
not knowing who they are

improvising on the horn
and the occasional sex is good too
love would be nice

the horror boring nights of TV are bad
a medication to sleep
so very dull, worse than any pill

all is about accepting the loneliness
when inspiration dies all is dead
all some jive uninteresting challenge

so death doesn't look so bad
the big forever vacation
the giving up of trying
the beautiful life
gone at last for good

the big surrender
the big i no longer give a fuck
about cars or homes or love or art
or romance or sex or friends
or fear or family or history

being done looks okay
back home into the nothingness
feels okay feels right
no big deal

all wanting and loneliness
is over
nice little meaningless deal
nice to let the flame go out

it has been a good party
endless sleep is good and heroic

good night
and sweet dreams

# Hernia

**At seven years old,** as I was getting out of the bathtub mother noticed one of my balls was hanging a lot lower than the other one. She called, "Joe, come and take a look at this," he did, both looking at my innocent balls. Dr. Lief was called, he came to the house the next day. I hid under the baby grand piano, scared, I felt no pain. Somehow they talked me out from under the piano, Dr. Lief, a good guy, took me into the upstairs bathroom, we did have three bathrooms. He shut off the light and put a flashlight behind my balls. A hernia! Fuck, memory so clear, over seventy years ago. Mom said I had to go to the hospital for an operation, of course I said no way. I was really freaked out. So she does this thing in front of me, she telephones the hospital and tells them she wants a room so she can stay with me, of course it was all bullshit. The next day we get to the hospital, a nurse sticks some needlelike thing in my finger, mom says, see you tomorrow and leaves!

**I'm in this ward with other kids,** I think rather than being freaked out my feeling was, fuck them, not the kids on the ward, my parents, let them kill me here in this hospital, the first of those feelings. The nurses and staff are pretty nice as I recall. A woman is giving me a pre-surgery enema, they must have given me something to relax me or make me sleepy, I remember feeling pretty good, my first experience being stoned, certainly not my last. Vague memory going down in an elevator on a gurney, I've had a claustrophobic fear of elevators to this very day. Don't remember much of my parents being there.

**The next day,** confined to bed, this nice little Italian kid
in the ward came over to talk. We'd gotten on to the subject
of God, (nice to have a recording of that, two seven-year-
olds discussing God). He says to me, he has a picture of God,
goes back to his bed and dresser and brings back a framed 8
by 10 picture of Christ on the cross, nails and all. Needless
to say I'm pretty taken aback! I had always pictured God as
this beautiful woman, maybe still do, not some naked bleeding
dead man nailed to a cross. I think I just said, no that's
not God, he said, yeah it is. You sure? Yeah I'm sure. I
stuck with the beautiful babe. Maybe I saw her in one of my
brother's skin mags

# Health Summary

Review this list of your current health issues in preparation for your upcoming visit. Please discuss any changes or new health issues with your provider. **Call 911 if you have an emergency.**

| | | |
|---|---|---|
| **Osteoarthrosis**<br>Added 1/6/2010 | **Mixed anxiety depressive disorder**<br>Added 1/6/2010 | **Elevated cholesterol**<br>Added 1/6/2010 |
| **Tobacco use disorder**<br>Added 1/6/2010 | **Alcohol abuse**<br>Added 1/6/2010 | **Chronic obstructive pulmonary disease**<br>Added 1/6/2010 |
| **Inguinal hernia**<br>Added 1/6/2010 | **Trigeminal nerve palsy**<br>Added 8/18/2017 | **Lipoma of abdominal wall**<br>Added 9/29/2017 |
| **CLL (chronic lymphocytic leukemia)**<br>Added 9/29/2017 | **Insomnia**<br>Added 9/29/2017 | **BPH (benign prostatic hyperplasia)** |

| Memory difficulty | Left shoulder pain | Elevated PSA |
| Added 10/25/2017 | Added 10/25/2017 | Added 12/11/2017 |

| Claudication | Healthcare maintenance | HTN (hypertension) |
| Added 10/3/2018 | Added 10/3/2018 | Added 1/7/2019 |

| Epidermoid cyst | Lung nodule |
| Added 1/7/2019 | Added 11/3/2019 |

MyChart® licensed from Epic Systems Corporation © 1999 - 2018

# Jr Collins

one night standing
in front of the five spot
with my childhood friend
joe moreno who played
french horn

waiting to hear monk

a beat up looking guy
with a beat up
french horn case
appears

we're sixteen
or seventeen years old

joe asked the guy
do you play french horn

he says
do you know who I am
no we don't

he says

I'm jr collins
fucking jr collins

and walked off
after asking
for a smoke

later we realized
he played on
the original
miles davis
birth of the cool

a few years later
I had much to do with him
on the lower east side

so burnt out on speed
yet brilliant
he'd walk around
with his works (needle)
behind his ear
like it was a pencil

I'd ask
junior do you
want to play

he'd say
I have to do
some soldering

he'd put his soldering iron
on the stove
and proceed
to do this strange soldering
on his horn

**50**

then he passed out
in the middle of
a sentence
right in the chair
he was sitting in

he'd been up for weeks

my dear friend victor
and I carried him into
victors bed
he slept for days

we'd check that
he wasn't dead
tried to give him water

he woke up days later
ready to go
like nothing happened

that's how genius goes

it has it's own desperation

jr was an interesting
soul with a big heart
great sense of humor
forgotten musician

the birth and death
of the cool

1/17/93

in this boiler room of truth
i sit on my own coffin
hammer in hand
hammer banging on my own head
to no jazz rhythm
to no four-four beat

I gang up on myself
with youthful energy
a street gang
with no football rules
or needle dealings

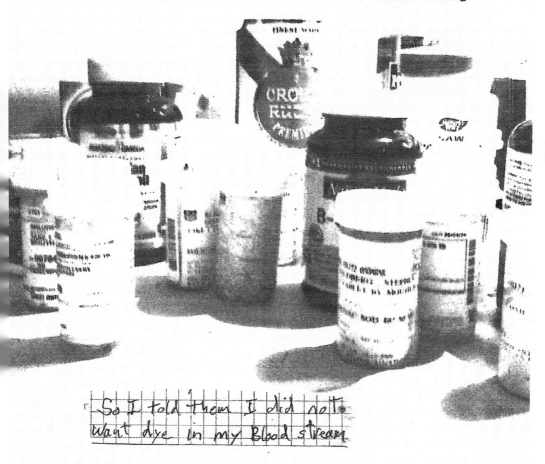

So I told them I did not
want dye in my blood stream

# FIGURING *Shit* OUT

Sometimes I get so sick of trying to figure **shit** out. I don't mean what to eat for dinner or what to wear (I wear the same thing everyday), or how to pay the bills, or whether to take a bath or shower, or what size font to use, get a dog or not. I mean big stuff, the big **shit**, "**shit**" not so bad a word, the waste that comes out of us. I mean life and death stuff, universal stuff, black hole stuff, infinity stuff, existence stuff. It gets tiring, yes sometimes exciting and sometimes frightening and confusing, sometimes beautiful, but exhausting. So I drink.

Now the alcohol turns off a part of the brain, and yes affects the coordination of the body while giving it a feeling of perfect comfort, not unlike a well built sofa or a tender embrace. The part of the brain it shuts down for me, is the "me" part, very close to nonexistence. And that feels so very good. Which might mean that nonexistence feels good. A nightly experiment. A nightly vacation for me.

I understand that drugs, alcohol included, have different effects on different people, even though we are 98% the same. If I was in another's perception, life would look pretty much the same. Just addicted to different concerns: am I fat and ugly, does my life have meaning, will my child die, how can i get money, am I dying, I lost my drivers license, will he/she leave me, the car needs an oil change and on and on.

I think, not sure, we have to put ourselves way out in the universe, get some distance about meaning and separation and our self importance. If our perception of reality died, would reality die, of course not. If you or I walked out of our safe little, or big, homes and got hit by a trailer truck and died, then if someone came into our home and turned the hot water faucet on, it would run hot water, regardless of our death. I have no idea what that means, the booze has had it's comfort effect, nice deal. I get it makes some sick, weed freaks me out, mostly we are the same. Arms, legs, heads, hair, eyes, brains, toes, fingers, sex slightly different, not much. More alike than not. That's pretty much it.

STEPHEN JAY GOLDBERG

52

# GRANDPA ALBERT E

4/09

the guy said
we're going to the beach
to smoke some pot
You want to come

no thanks
I don't like pot
it overstimulates
the frontal cortex
the one I need a vacation from

I'm a downer guy
I always need to come down
and pot fucks up
my non concept of time

**like my grandpa
Albert E said to me
don't fuck with time
and it won't fuck with you
stick to the bicycle**

I said to him
**e=mc squared
he said, can I use that?**
I said, sure
I was only three at the time
he had such a nice smile

what I meant was
**my mother, Edna = mac and cheese
out of the square box**
he took it the wrong way
he gave me a Hershey bar
and a nickel
they gave us
Hiroshima

I liked when
he put me on the handlebars
and later played the violin for me
little did we know
they would dissect his brain
and try to figure out
what genius was

The DNA in the E-brain
read simply
no big deal, followed by NBD
but they made the bomb anyway
the creation of deformities
burnt flesh and hybrids
no, he didn't invent the Prius

he told me on his deathbed
music is the best humanity can do
and he didn't mean rock'n roll
though he would have liked
Chuck Berry and free flowing Bob Dylan

I have his violin
in the refrigerator
I wish they'd stop
slicing up his brain

**Edna (my mother) = macaroni and cheese
in a square box**
he got that rectangles
are just variations
on the square

thanks Grandpa
for the bike ride
they never once
looked in your heart
I've given your violin
to my daughter, your great granddaughter
she makes it sing

**love you, Papa E
the sad, sad eyes
and the beautiful smile
see you in heaven**

as you said
God does not play dice with the universe
but I bet
he or she plays
chess
and I know you always mate him

so we made the bomb
a-bomb, h-bomb
the end-all bomb
we will set it off
and at last end humanity
the pain, the suffering
the inhumanity, the greed
the selfishness

and in a thousand years
the flower and butterfly
will start again
and in ten thousand years
we'll come out of the sea again
with tails and gills
and tiny prehensile legs

and give it another shot
breathing air
and in a hundred thousand years
back to e=mc squared
mac and cheese

on the shelf
of the nearest
satan's price chopper
with ten thousand brands
of mac and cheese
and a hundred thousand
breakfast cereals

huge colosseums of choice
them pushing their carts
frozen refrigerator brands
with giant bellies
impossible to find their sex
amongst their folds

another jew-christ is crucified
for being thin
and on it goes
for another hundred thousand years

we'll never get it right
until alligators are
the highest life form
**just stop it there**

**please**

STEPHEN JAY GOLDBERG

**56**

# A DREAM
## Can Be

a dream can be
**trouble**
dissipate power
waste time
the "if only's"
wait for
the recycling truck

mixed cardboard
egg shells
plane tickets
melting in
new born snow

a daughter's visit
freezing
into an ice sculpture
of fire and smoke
and snow snakes

black words play games
on white pixel screens
flying like birds
through the innocent air

a voice says
you can't miss something you never had
the answer comes
in a pelicans beak,
you've had it baby
you had too much of it

don't call me baby
okay baby

are we playing millionaire
or be good to yourself
or is it match game
or survivor
or family feud

the game remains unknown

# a tough guy falls

9/22/08

FOR MY FRIEND, PETER FREYNE

(published in *SEVEN DAYS* after his death)


it's hard to see a tough guy fall
we're all so delicate
we just hang on to this life
by a spiders thread

THERE YOU LAY
TONIGHT
IN ROOM 466
UNABLE TO SPEAK
LOOKING PALE LIKE WHITE MARBLE

something pressing on
your brain
who knows how long
it was waiting

YOU THE OUTSPOKEN ONE
THE ONE THE POLITICOES FEARED
AND THE PUBLIC EXCITED TO READ

you were a bad bar drunk
loud, insulting and nasty
but you quit the booze
years ago
you quit the smokes
years ago

YOU GOT YOURSELF A BICYCLE
AND YES A HELMET
TO PROTECT THAT ACTIVE BRAIN
THE ATTACK NOW
COMES FROM INSIDE

the inside track
the inside attack

YOU TOLD ME
YOU WANTED CHANGE
POLITICS NO LONGER INTERESTED YOU
YOU WERE LOOKING INSIDE
THE VAST INSIDE
SO BRAVE TO GIVE UP
WHAT YOU LOVED
AND WHAT
YOU WERE LOVED FOR

you gave up the bicycle
and helmet
you said
it no longer interested you

WE EXCHANGED
LOVING TOUGH GUY EMAILS
YOU SAID YOU WANTED
TO WRITE A PLAY

there is no lesson
it gets each
and every one of us
sooner or later

YES IT WAS HARD TO
WALK INTO THAT HOSPITAL
YET AGAIN
HARD TO SEE YOU HELPLESS
UNABLE TO SPEAK

you knew i was there
and got it
we looked into
each others eyes
and both smiled

IT COULD BE ME
OR ANYONE OF US
YOU GRASPED MY HAND
STILL STRONG

unsaid;
it is what it is
that's the deal

YOU WOULD HAVE LAUGHED
I GOT LOST
TRYING TO FIND THE HOSPITAL
THAT I KNOW AND DREAD
ONLY TOO WELL
WE TOUGH GUYS
FALL HARD
AND GET UP AT THE
EIGHT COUNT

sometimes yes
sometimes not
so delicate is
that spider thread

NO LESSON
JUST CARING
AND YES
IT DOES TAKE A TOUGH GUY
TO CARE, REALLY CARE

we are not our brains
we are not our bodies
we are not our politics
we are not our philosophy
we are not our possessions
we are not our children
we are not the cancers
that eat our brains

THE DEAL IS NO DEAL
THE BEST WE CAN DO IS CARE

a spider has a short delicate life

LOVE, S

# EXOTIC creature

I'm sure you saw that, such a beautiful exotic
creature, bigger than a mouse, smaller than a
drug addict, so very graceful. Did you see it? It
doesn't matter, I saw it.

ALL THIS JIVE
ABOUT FINDING
YOUR OWN TRUTH

REALIZE
WE ARE ONLY
LITTLE TINY
MEANINGLESS ANTS

ONLY BIG DEALS
TO OURSELVES
OVERGROWN EGOS
REFLECTIONS IN IDIOT MIRRORS

DO WE REALLY WANT
AN ENDLESS NEVER ENDING
GREAT FUCK

ALL THE REST IS BUSY WORK

AND FRUSTRATION
A WASTE OF TIME

A WASHED DISH
HAS NO MEANING
EXCEPT TO DIRTY

We never can forget that we are animals with brains
and clothing and sex and symphony orchestras and
wars and books and doctors, the power of the
unforgivable need to reproduce forgives everything.

# S t o n e

In the late spark
of cool energy
in oppressive heat
oppressive humidity

the sump pump
pissing water from
the basement of what was a home
I wasn't meant
to live in alone

**I get that everything**
**In the universe**
**is accidental**

some random shit
that we will never understand
it overworks the primal brain
the intellect is like
a sink of dirty dishes

which one to wash first
make clean, exciting
make each dirty dish
important, caring
connecting the physical
to the emotions and night dreams

**I get that I am an animal**
**given this gift of life**
**with it's pain and passion**

no more evolved
then this ancient stone
I found and studied
on the lake-side beach

random, so very beautiful
thousands of years old
holding so tight in my hand
every detail perfect

**it makes me question**
**what it is to be an artist**
**never being more perfect**
**than this ancient stone**

the human conscious mind
is not as interesting as the history
of this stone, just sitting in the water
so innocent, worn, and yes suffering
with it's gorgeous lines of wear

Samuel Beckett would often
refer to sucking stones
a stone in the mouth
to taste the flying of time
very un-chewing gum

**I have not yet put the stone**
**in my mouth, even though**
**I think it could save me**
**connect to the all and every-thing**

wanting is trouble
need is heartbreaking
for all that pretend to care

so keep the stone
under the tongue
if you swallow
it will kill you
even if it feels like
the right thing to do

to eat the stone and chew
breaking the seven
teeth I have left
to surrender the ego
and the neediness

and be free
like the giant birds
that float the thermals
with no effort

**I feel so very alone**
**always feel better**
**after talking to you**

you have your life
I have mine
we try not to interrupt or invade

and learn and discover
I so much feel like you understand
even when you don't hear me
or your eyes look lost
and a bit tired

**I love the fact that**
**you do your best**
**to be there, pay attention**
**I really so much need that**

thank you, Stephen

# Grammar School

My friend Paul Canus lived right across the street from the school PS 144. I'd often cut class, I guess starting around seventh grade when departmental started, meaning rather than staying in one room all day, we went from class to class. So it gave me a chance to get out of there, like I said I'd go over to Paul's house, hang out, smoke cigarettes and have cocktails. Needless to say one day I got caught, sent to the principal's office. He called my mother, told her I had cut class, I remember him saying "Mrs Goldberg, I think Stephen clearly seems to smell from gin." I think I was suspended for a few days. My friends all called me "Goldie," later "Rocky."

I was by sixth grade in the school band, not clear on the dates, so the band was on stage and the principal Mr. Pearlberg, we called him Pearlballs, was giving a speech. I thought I'd give him a trumpet accompaniment, kind of a poetry and jazz thing. He turned around and in front of the whole school, yelled, "What, do you have rocks in your head?" We thought it was pretty funny and after that I was know as "Rocky."

We "bad kids" were always placed in the last seats of the rows of seats. One day during class my friend Whitey calls over, "Goldie" and he has his cock out with a hard-on, we both crack up. Another time in assembly, the whole school in the PS 144 auditorium, my buddy Joey Aqualina, we called him Gargalina, pointed down to his pants. Inside his pants his cock was pulsating in time to the student body singing the Star Spangled Banner.

# miles
## *davis*

i saw and heard you
play so many times

i sat next to you
at the bar in the village vanguard
i said hey miles
maybe you thought
***there's that white kid again***

you gave me that look
**that miles look**
your dark eyes
into my dark eyes
no words

you played your ass off that night
with **tony williams**
**herbie hancock**
**ron carter** and **wayne shorter**

it wasn't jazz
it was drama
dangerous, interesting
filled with power
and tenderness

you played one of those
screaming pained licks
a guy at the front table
stood up
couldn't control himself

and screamed
"yeah miles"
**you just looked at him**
**like you looked at me**
as if to say
what's the big deal
i'm miles davis
and you're not
so calm down

he always dressed great
always looked cool
he wasn't just a trumpet player
**he was miles davis**
a style of a man

he lived on the upper west side
73rd street, i lived on 93rd street

a friend of mine
an okay trumpet player
but good band arranger
was playing in this shitty
little bar on 72nd and broadway

he told me miles walked in one night
stoned
and asked if he could play don's horn
a conn constellation
**don said miles was so stoned**
**he could hardly make a sound**

another friend who lived
on miles' block
said he found miles
sitting on his stoop
at 3am
and miles asked him to
take him uptown to cop some coke

68

he did
who wouldn't

**when a man is a genius**
**we have to take care of him**
it's our responsibility

a locksmith i knew
went to fix up
miles' security system in his house
he described miles as a crocodile
crawling on the floor
then the power comes
after and because
of the crawling
and helplessness

**yeah he shot junk**
**played with charlie parker**
when he was 19
telling his parents
he was at julliard
school of music

never had the chops of dizzy
but he had the soul
and art of a picasso

he quit playing
for a year or two
and shot rats and other things
through a rooftop in paris

i'd take the bus uptown
after a subway ride
from queens
to manhattan school of music

there were two shoe stores
one miles, the other davis
right next door to each other
on third avenue

i'd always smile
at those signs
those shoe stores
on my way to learn the
theory of music

i don't like having heroes
**but, the big but is**
**how much i love miles davis**
on bad nights that sound
kept me alive
in a rat-bat infested house

so miles
thank you
for your inspiration
and that sound
and the space you leave
for the rhythm
section and music to breathe
thank you
for unspoken teaching
dead is not dead
**thank you miles davis**

*thank you*

STEPHEN JAY GOLDBERG

**70**

# 10TH STREET MORNING

9/17/15

I'M LIVING AT MY FRIEND BILLY'S, WEST 10TH STREET PLACE in the Village, he was gone to parts unknown, a great guitar player. It was a little one room place, nice, yeah it's okay. I had been doing "the program," seeing this woman who was the bartender at Cafe Central and a few others. I'm in my early 40's or late 30's, never good at dates. I'll figure those things out sometime, you know, put things in order. In memories it doesn't matter much. Like dreams.

I had broken up with H a little time before, what a drama that was. So I'm having a slip, up all night alone, drinking and taking pills, the sun is out on West 10th.

I call H up in Westchester, I'm feeling really bad. I had bought myself a rabbit skin fur coat that had left rabbit hair all over my black clothes, I also painted Billy's wooden floor glossy black.

As I'm talking to H, I'm messing around with a razor blade on my wrist, drama queen that I am, stoned as I am. I tell her what I'm doing and how I wanted to come home, be with her and my son. I'm going on and on and she stays on the phone. I'm the one who fucked it all up.

Now there seems to be more blood on the phone and on the newly painted floor. I am kind of enjoying it, I'm not proud of this shit, not at all.

After what seems like forever, still on the phone, there's a knock on the door. I ask, who's there? A nice gentle male voice says, "Steve, open the door, it's the New York Police Department, please open the door." There is more blood, not deep vein blood, but blood. I tell her to hold on. I open the door and there are two nice New York uniformed cops. I was glad to have some company. They said something like, "How are you doing?" I might have said something like, "Not so good."

They ask me to hang up the phone, I did, I think I said goodby. They gently take me over to St. Vincent's Hospital, a few blocks away, I had been drinking hard and taking pills since the night before. I don't remember if we were in a black and white or walked, I would think it was the car. These New York cops seemed so nice and understanding, like they got it. In those days these guys are the best.

I'm in the ER feeling okay, nice to be with people. Some parts are understandably vague. As they say, I feel no pain.

This young Puerto Rican intern says he's going to sew up my wrist. I ask him, "Is this going to hurt?" Our eyes meet and we both start to laugh, I mean really crack up, really laugh hard. Like for both of us it was the funniest thing ever, it was pretty funny.

So he puts the stitches in, no they didn't hurt. I thank him. I have a nice white bandage on my wrist. I think the police are still hanging out.
Then this very serious doctor says to me, I think you should see someone on the psych ward. I tell him I don't think so, how the guy who sewed me up fixed me. Which he did. The joke was on me, on us. Everyone was so nice. I guess I just needed a little attention.

I remember walking out of there on West 10th Street, feeling so good in the bright sunlight. Learning a lesson I still don't understand or who to thank. I might have bought myself a big breakfast, I don't remember. I did return the rabbit skin fur coat.

That next night my friend Neal came over and the babe from Cafe Central, we had some drinks, or I had some drinks, Neal left and the babe and I had a nice time.

S.G

# BiCyCle

years, lifetimes ago
i rode my son
on a bicycle
through the streets of
the upper west side of new york
taking him to day care

> I told him keep your feet in
> so they don't get caught in the spokes
> he said, I know dad,
> you don't have to keep telling me

the next day I didn't tell him
his foot got caught in the spokes
on west end avenue

> just like the car door
> I'd say watch your fingers
> as I closed the car door
> he said dad
> you don't have to
> keep telling me

so I didn't and his little fingers
got caught in the car door
nothing broken, just some heavy tears

> maybe he was thinking
> why didn't you remind me
> about the car door
> why do you listen to a kid

I built the bike I have now
at earl's schwinn
I worked there building bikes
I got paid by the bike

I was so slow at it
the guys in the taiwan factory
most likely
made more money
than I did

so far in the past
so much has happened
far too much to talk about
to render in words

like a huge pile
of overripe firewood
almost too old to burn
it will produce no heat
only tears, the anti-fire agent

heartbeat strong
yet broken
blood pressure perfect
pulse beating as it should be
strong legs, forever pedaling

the smooth ride

my first bike an english racer
rudge, or was it rugby
it was the less of the two
the cheaper one
dad always getting
the less expensive one

hey the freedom was amazing
the little click of the gears
a tabla rhythm,
before I knew about tablas
or upbeats and downbeats
or cigarettes and women

breeze on lips
power in legs
all was good

## Alcohol

My God, not that I have a God, alcohol has been everything to me, it turns off the brain, or shuts off the babble, makes the stupid honest brain take charge, the brain, head shit that has shut down for years. Of course I am what is called an alcoholic because of the amount I drink every night. No big deal as the raindrops fall.

mom

Dad

Brother

I wasn't Born

```
          and the seventh floor men
          piss and throw up and drink
          last nights warm flat beer
          and don't even wonder who
          missed what and never hear
          of anything or kissed a
          beautiful woman and never will

          the car doesn't come


tiny plaster casts on broken rose stems in mothers vase
in an over stylisa over rated polished floor contrived loft


          old smelly men with beer and cigarettes .
          .dance the same  mantra

          there's more truth in their
          glazed eyes as they watch
          the vertical hold  flicker
          on their tin foiled aerieled  t.v.s

than tight assed women squeezed into seventy-five dollar
jeans that outline their frigid cunts.
```

# Chess

11/19/2019

always four games at once
sadly online
yes with humans
all over the world

haven't played with
physical pieces
in a long time
it would be nice

I don't know anyone
who plays chess
my grandchildren
play soccer

I did teach my son
and grandson
to play chess

son gave it up
grandson prefers
computer games
soon he'll prefer girls
we do play every
now and then

the king has limited moves
one square at a time
the queen can
move almost any place

MAYBE THE INVENTORS
OF CHESS
UNDERSTOOD SOMETHING
ABOUT
MALE FEMALE RELATIONSHIPS

how strong the queen is
how limited the king is
one box at a time

once the king dies
game over
checkmate
death to all

A BRILLIANT GAME
REFLECTING LIFE
FOOTBALL
WITH THE PAIN OF THE
INTELLECT

I went to join
a chess club
with real pieces
real people

it was everything
to them
it is a beautiful game

better with real pieces
too hard for me
to deal with
the chess club

WITH CLOCKS
AND REAL PIECES
NOT ONE WOMAN THERE

they had
little cases
that contained their sets
almost like musician's instrument cases

the main guy
huge belly
hanging over
his belt

the chess players
with real pieces
all ranked
amongst themselves

it all seemed so hopeless
I lost a few games
with real pieces
and left

it is a beautiful game
need to find a friend
who enjoys
playing with real pieces

ASHTRAY ON THE TABLE
CIGARETTES AND LIGHTER
NICE CHILLED COCKTAILS
CLASSICAL MUSIC ON THE STEREO
TIME TO THINK A FEW MOVES AHEAD

NO RUSH AS THE RAIN FALLS

# NAT
## PAVONE

Nat Pavone's name appears on Maynard Ferguson albums
**lead trumpet Nat Pavone**
at 17 Nat was the hottest lead trumpet player in New York

**You could get a trumpet at 10 years old**
**practice 10 hours a day for 10 years**
**and never be able to do what Nat could do**

Maynard could do it at 16
he just had it
played lead for Stan Kenton
they called it screech trumpet
high notes that could blow the ice caps
off the north and south poles
believe me it's hard

I got hired to play a rock and roll review
at the Philadelphia Civic Center
thousands of people
I was hired to play trumpet and trombone
Nat was the lead trumpet player
the sax player drove us to Philly from New York

we played a little rehearsal
without the stars
Little Richard, Chuck Berry and the rest
the charts were all screwed up
but we did okay

Nat told me he had
just gotten out of the hospital
he didn't say for what
I figured it was detox
he looked kind of bloated

I had played with him in a big band in NY
and knew he was drinking cheap wine
and on the methadone program
chipping smack when he could

he was a sweet guy
and played the crappy music so well
big fat strong sound
for all the jive rock and roll acts
we were all there for the money
we did the rehearsal real fast
and played the first show
all went well

In the break between shows
drinks were served to the band and acts

**the second show Nat was all fucked up
couldn't play a note**
put the mute where the mouthpiece goes
the band leader Billy Vera
looking at me yelling, "Get him out of here!"
I look at Billy, shrugging my shoulders
putting my arm around Nat who's spinning out
and play Nat's trumpet parts

Then Little Richard comes out
the crowd goes nuts
Nat runs center stage with Little Richard
twirling his trumpet and dancing
the security cops grab him and toss him off stage
I finish the gig on trumpet

STEPHEN JAY GOLDBERG

80

after the gig Nat is unconscious backstage
we check that he's alive
he's okay, he's breathing
Billy pays us
no money for Nat
there's a big argument about paying Nat
we say he played the rehearsal and the first show
we get some of his money and carry him into the car

coming out of the tunnel into the city
Nat who passed out in the front seat
wakes up and says to the saxophone player
"I don't think I'm going to work for those guys anymore"
the sax player says
"Nat, I don't think you have to worry about it"

We drop Nat off in the Village
so he can cop and get high

**Nat died a few months later**
**methadone, smack and cheap wine**
**never made 40**
**God bless him**

he wore a cape
and had a beautiful wife from Sweden
he was a monster trumpet player
ask Maynard, ask any trumpet player
his innocence killed him


## NAT PAVONE

# smoking

some smoke, some drink, some shoot dope
some overeat, some are yogis
but she says, the smoking stinks
introduced by the American Indian

there are very few things
that have stuck with me
from the age of twelve
not parents, not friends, not wives
not lovers, not brothers,
cigarettes are still here

when Jay was dying at Sloan Kettering
in New York, i helped him into the
visitors lounge, he asked for a smoke

i said, Jay it's not good for you
he said, who gives a fuck
i'm dying
we had a smoke together
i helped him back to his bed
like an Indian ritual
how very much i loved him

it sounds crazy
but cigarettes are the only constant
things that haven't given up on me
nor have i given up on them

to me they are not poison
but old friends, rolling them
with my dear friend Victor
on Stanton Street

        so please babe, don't be too hard on me
        about this, it does have a history
        a 60 year old history
        it hasn't killed me yet, nor will it

you light a match, suck the smoke in
like an old forgiving friend
easy, simple, somehow it stimulates the brain
like an old black and white movie

        i don't want to stink up your beautiful home
        but this might be bigger

love you bigger than you might need
        ...stephen

# CITY BIRDS

IT WAS A LOOK OUT OF THE LEFT CORNER OF MY RIGHT EYE.
She was coming up out of the subway stairs at Columbus Circle, I was
sitting there watching the winged birds, wondering why do they live in
this city and if they know happiness. City birds. I was thinking, take a
suite at the Plaza, so what if I have no money, neither do the pigeons.

Now she had this strap over her shoulder that separated her breasts,
it hung right between them, defining this is the right one, this is the left
one. I figured there were books in the bag, yet she was too old to be a
student, maybe just a reader. The books outlined her blue bag the way
the strap outlined her bra-less small breasts. So yes, there was something
about her.

Everyday I would sit there at Columbus Circle watching the people
flow out of the subway. Wondering where they were rushing to get to.
After the war, I had no place to get to, nothing to kill.

I knew she was the one, with her strap of books and the innocent look
in her eyes behind her glasses. How do you go up to a strange woman and
tell her, she's the one, the only one. It was the same pounding in my heart
when I killed men in the war. Except with them there were no questions
about communication. It was the same as taking that killing shot. It had
never happened before and it was not something I was waiting for. She
was the one. My heart about to beat out of my chest.

I walked behind her, three people between us. She was walking
uptown along the park, I was more frightened than when I saw my buddy
Tommy get blown up in the war. What do I do, what do I say, I can't lose
her, I can't frighten her. My voice going down my throat. It has been so
long since I spoke to a woman, except Sherry the bartender on upper
Broadway. I had said, "a double bourbon." I can't say that to this woman
who I am in love with. She is perfect, innocent to the killing. If I lose her,
all is lost and I will die of loneliness. I don't know what to say or what to
do, I'm shaking, my hands are sweating, like when I killed the first one.
It was an order, shoot to kill. And I did. A shot through the head. What
do I say to her.

She made a left turn on 73rd Street and took out her keys, I knew it was now that I had to say something, she is the one, the only one, how can I feel this deep love for a woman i don't know.

Her back was perfect. The way she presented the keys, the way her hands moved, like my fingers on the trigger when I killed them all, the enemy.

I said, with a choked throat, "Excuse me, but I think I know you, a friend of my sister Jane."

I have no sister or brothers. She turned with those burning black eyes and said,

"So you're Jane's long lost brother who was in the the war."

"Yes that's me," my God, waiting to wake up from the bombs and blood.

She took the keys out of the downstairs door, turned and looked at me, really looked into me.

"Jane has told me so much about you. About the war."

"Yeah, Jane and I are close."

"She showed me your letters, I hope that's okay."

"Yeah, it's okay."

"I'm Sarah, but you know that, Jane must have written about me."

"Yes she did."

"Would you like to come up for some tea."

Now, I have no sister Jane, I don't drink tea, but I love this innocent woman, I didn't know her name. But I remember hearing her voice when I was shot through the calf, she said, "You'll be okay." As she was fixing the wound. A nurse. Hardly any blood, just pain. Till I went unconscious.

I could hardly speak by that 73rd Street doorway. I said, "No thank you, I don't drink tea."

The words came from below my feet, below the NY cement, up from the spinning earth.

I managed to say, "I'd like to see you again, I live at the Plaza."

"Sarah, my name is Sarah, I know you have forgotten, it's okay."

Then she, Sarah, I had forgotten, she took a pen and little note pad out of her book bag, wrote something down and handed it to me. Like the shell through the calf. I could feel the wound and it's pain. Bloodless. The downstairs door closed, she disappeared. My finger off the trigger.

Rants Raves & Ricochets

85

I walked and walked and walked. Went to the West End Bar, there was Sherry, I order a double bourbon, sucked it down, she poured me another. She said, "No charge Cal, you look a little pale."

I felt the neat folded piece of paper in my pants pocket, it was burning, like the grenade that blew Louie away, his guts all over me. Internal parts of the human body. I can't face another war, or another bleeding man, even if that man is me.

Football on the TV, with the sound off, the power of men, strong men, made me realize I was nothing except a killer of the enemy, the music on the jukebox didn't fit with the semi-violence on the TV. Why didn't they just shoot each other but no, this is sport.

I could feel the note paper rubbing on my thigh, above the calf that the bullet had gone through. It was a new pain.

It read, "Cal, let's meet for coffee, I'll have tea, you have coffee or your drink of choice, I'd like us to talk, my number is 212-862-9845, Jane says hello. She does miss you. I understand detachment."

Again, I have no sister, no sister Jane, I had to say something, I was on the spot for words. Why did she do that, she must have a boyfriend or a cat or dog, something. How did she know my name, Cal. The way she said it, Cal, all dragged out, and the way she said "detachment," like a musical phrase. No I couldn't go up there and have tea.

Upon my release from the army, the paper said I was of sound mind and had done great service to my country. Meaning killing those Korean fuckers, who I didn't know at all. I knew they were trying to kill me, so it was okay to shoot them. Yeah I was a good shot, it must have come from the piano lessons mother wanted me to have. Be accurate, hit the right notes, through the head.

What was her name? Think. "Sherry, another bourbon." Yeah, yeah, Sarah, like a dream, I had dreamt about her in the Korean freezing mud. Kill or be killed. I even saw that book bag, strap separating her breasts, separating the life and death of the mud moment. I know, or think I know I'm not nuts or shell shocked.

I pull the burning piece of paper out of my pants pocket. It says 212-862-9845, that's all. The script is clear and graceful. Too late to call. Maybe tomorrow. Yeah, tomorrow.

# THE MOVIE star

ALWAYS WANTED
TO BE A BUM
HOPELESS
WITH
NO THOUGHT
OF FUTURE

KNOWING AS
A CHILD
ALL WAS
WITHOUT HOPE

THAT IS A COMFORT
SAFE

WHY STRUGGLE
TO MAKE A WAY
IN THIS HOPELESS LIFE

YET I BECAME FAMOUS
AND RICH
WHY
SIMPLE

BECAUSE
I WAS
VERY GOOD LOOKING
REALLY GOOD LOOKING

FRIENDS GAVE ME MONEY
TO GO TO HOLLYWOOD
THEY INVESTED

I WAS OKAY
ON THE FISHING BOAT

WE DRANK AND JOKED
I SAID
SORRY
I WAS BORN LIKE THIS

I GOT A ROOM
HUNG OUT
IN THE FAMOUS
HOLLYWOOD
DRUGSTORE

THIS GUY ASKED
ARE YOU AN ACTOR
YEAH I AM
NO I WAS A FISHERMAN

THEY TOOK SOME PHOTOS
TOLD ME TO
SAY MY NAME

THEN I'M IN A MOVIE
ALL I HAVE TO DO
IS KISS A BEAUTIFUL
WOMAN
EASY

THEY GAVE ME
A FEW HUNDRED BUCKS

*I GOT CALLED BACK*

THE DIRECTOR SAYS
YOU KISS THIS BABE
A GUY COMES IN
AND SHOOTS YOU

STEPHEN JAY GOLDBERG

88

YOU FALL DOWN DEAD
CAN YOU DO THAT
SURE EASY
THEY GIVE ME
THREE GRAND

*I GOT CALLED BACK*

THE DIRECTOR SAYS
YOU LOOK IN THIS
BABE'S EYES
YOU SAY
I LOVE YOU HONEY

SHE WILL START TO CRY
YOU STROKE HER HAIR
AND YOU SAY I LOVE YOU
THEN YOU KISS HER

A GUY COMES IN
AND FAKE HITS YOU
ON THE HEAD
WITH A BREAKAWAY CHAIR

CAN YOU DO THAT

YEAH EASY
THEY GIVE ME
TEN GRAND

*I GOT CALLED BACK*

THEY GIVE ME SOME PAPERS
WORDS HIGHLIGHTED
WITH A YELLOW MARKER
JUST A FEW

THE BABE KISSES ME
AND SAYS I'M SO AFRAID
I SAY DON'T WORRY
A GUY COMES IN
I SHOOT HIM

THEY GIVE ME
THIRTY GRAND

AND ON IT WENT
A HUNDRED GRAND

MORE WORDS
MORE KISSING
BEAUTIFUL WOMEN
MORE MONEY

WHAT CAN I SAY
BORN TO BE
GOOD LOOKING

I WOULDN'T CALL IT ACTING
JUST GOOD FORTUNE

YEAH I ENJOYED IT

NOW I'M OLD
LIVE IN THE HILLS
WATCH THE BIRDS
AT THE FEEDERS

*NOT TOO SHABBY*

# The eyepiece

the eye piece, then the
zipper, then the clutch,
then the spelling, the
recorder, the filter, then
the pipes, then the hot
water heater, then the back,
then the picture tube, the
B string, then the shutter,
the exhaust, the amp, the
teeth, the oil burner, the
steering box, the volume
control, the H on the type
writer, then the lids, the
oven, the long lens, the
master fader, the contrast,
the left speaker, then your
mother, your dog, the automatic
rewind, the rear window, the
liver, the hands, glasses,
socks, dimmer, sound post,
first valve, wide angle,
hinge, dried out, too damp,
too deep, too hot, too cold,
gasket, rings, telephone cord,
out of luck, mice, termites,
headlight, no light, kidney,
lung, brain, heart, woman, wrong
word, wrong turn, wrong map,
wrong street, wrong direction,
sheets, pillow, knee pad, no flint,
dinner, dinner, dinner, dinner,
fork, EAT.

# HOUSE WRECKERS
## *and*
# Mind Fuckers

T hey said they were bad, don't trust them, keep away from them. You know how drug addicts are. Whatever you do, don't give them any money. Don't let them know where you live. They will never leave, you'll end up leaving.

Not that it was a fancy place, Clinton Street and Houston Street, the lower East Side of New York. Me and my dear pal Victor Lichardello. Fellow trumpet players. In high school they called him Victor lick the Jell-O. In his old Brooklyn neighborhood. We're in our place, third floor walk-up. Six rooms, $65 a month. We had a hard time getting it together.

There's a knock on the door.

Three guys, known as the house wreckers and mind fuckers, street guys but good brilliant crazed guys. They said we brought you guys a gift. At least ten huge cases of lettuce. Piled up in the hallway outside our door. What the fuck are we going to do with all this lettuce? They said salads, or take a bath in it.

It's true we didn't have much to eat. Two of them left, (this is true shit I'm writing about). So yeah, we accepted the gracious gift and thanked them. Piled the many wooden cartons in our small kitchen. Junior helped and remained.

His name was Junior Collins, he played the French horn, jazz French horn, he's on the legendary Miles Davis recording, *Birth of the Cool*. He had been a junkie, heroin, but the whole gang, there must have been eight or ten of them, switched to speed, shooting it. It made them happy, like innocent children.

They collected things, anything they could find on the streets of New York, carried all the stuff around in many shopping bags. Junior kept his works (needle) behind his ear like a pencil. Not a worry in the world.

One of us asked him if he wanted to play some music. Both Victor and

I played trumpet. Junior always had his French horn with him, he said he had a bit of soldering to do. He put an old-fashioned soldering iron on the stove till it got really hot, it no longer looked like a French horn, he had done so much soldering on it. Speed, intravenous speed makes you do shit like that.

So he soldered and talked in the gentle speed whisper talk, really interesting, he knew everything about music and jazz and the street life. Then he sat down and asked for a glass of water. I asked him if he wanted some lettuce, we had a lot of it. He said no thanks, it's for you guys.

Then in the middle of the sentence he fell asleep in the chair. He had been up and walking the streets for weeks. So we let him sleep and we smoked our beautiful hand rolled Bugler cigarettes. After a few hours we tried to wake him, no go. Passed out on the kitchen chair. We didn't know if he was okay or what. We dragged him, helped him into Victor's bed, he too was a good guy, a great friend.

Junior slept for two and a half or three days. He woke like nothing was wrong. See you later. Junior, he didn't even piss in the chair or bed.

I had asked Junior about one of his buddies, Tony Frucella, a truly genius jazz trumpet player. No one in this world plays like him. I asked how Tony could play so well after serving so much jail time.

He said, pedal tones, you research it and try to understand. Tony made one beautiful album.

My brother Jay got me that album for my 16th birthday. It still blows me away.

I met Tony one night hanging out in the circle in Washington Square Park. It went like this:

"So Tony, how are you doing?"

"Yeah okay."

"Are you playing any place."

"Yeah, I play every night in Riverside Park."

Then he said, "I got arrested for jerking off in public. I told the judge, it's my dick."

I will never forget that conversation. The man was a true genius on the horn. Nobody like him.

The great white hope when all the greats were black. I heard stories about him sitting in with Charlie Parker. People would ask to sit in to play one of these difficult Bird tunes. Bird would say fine, let's do it in D flat, and Tony was the only one who could cut it. Mulligan tried to hire him but he was too difficult. One bad ass, Tony was.

Junior Collins was a brilliant and loving man, with a great sense of humor, and yeah he taught me a lot. About music and life. More than most. I miss those days, those days of the House Wreckers and Mind Fuckers.

I can still see him sitting in that kitchen chair, lovingly soldering his French horn, works behind his ear. Offering wisdom for the taking, surrounded by crates of lettuce.

Victor and I rolling Bugler cigarettes. "It was the best of times and the worst of times."

I need to live for all that was passed on to me, by the House Wreckers and Mind Fuckers. So I can give that gift back to anyone that will take it.

So much more to tell.

**Goldberg**                                              9/22/15

# My

This guy, i don't want to say his name,
so this guy who was
taking care of the place I stayed in Mexico
a great chess player

He spent 8 years in jail
and played every day
besides doing all these other jail hustles

The first night we met
we knew we trusted each other
he asked to borrow some money
I gave him 50 pesos

He went out and copped some heroin
he came back fast and did himself in the vein
he asked if I wanted a hit, I said no,
even though I did,
I did want a hit but not from the works in his arm
it would have been like a bonding thing

He looked like a guy who could be frightening,
american-mexican,
a big belly and a tough badass look in his eye
he was sort of my mexican bodyguard
we would joke about that

If I got too drunk after playing
he would help me home
and make sure nobody stole my trumpet
I'd buy him a few beers, some smokes
I never felt used nor did he
he would always pay me back
he looked out for me

The chess games were amazing
I'd win once in awhile,
it just takes a little fuck up,
not looking at the whole board the whole picture

He'd move fast
I'd take my time
while he waited
he'd make this little
sucking sound through his teeth

I'd be three moves ahead
he'd be four moves ahead
we'd play and smoke cigarettes

he was a beautiful man, kind, strong
built like a tank, close to the ground
I wouldn't want to mess with him
if he wanted sex he'd pay for it
and that was more than okay with him

We were from different worlds,
he told me he had killed people,
had a piece (a gun), had a habit,
would fall asleep with his tv on,
and would clean the pool
so it was nice for my morning swim

He taught me a lot
about friendship, prison
about trust, addiction
about loneliness,
most of all about chess,
being fearless
about trading queens and losing it all
trapping the king, who can hardly move
only one square in any direction
he dies
the game is over

mate

STEPHEN JAY GOLDBERG

96

1/4/19

**strip**

**Club**

**Gig**

I had this great gig
43d street NYC
playing with this cool
jazz quintet
in a topless club

we could play
whatever we wanted
as long as it had a beat
and the girls
could dance to it

it was fun
and paid okay

at this point
I have no memory
who was in the band

I do remember
hanging out
in the girls
dressing room

easy subway ride
back to east ninth street

no I never did
any of the girls
it was work
and hanging out

then I get this call
from the manager
of this real famous band
do I want to work with them

I'm thinking
give up the topless gig
why
for what

we're playing good music
watching nice bouncing
tits and ass
getting paid okay
the perfect gig

the famous band paid
much better
they bought me new horns
the music okay
not my kind of music
but good

the horn parts
not very interesting
but I guess I did them
okay

the famous band guys
were good humble guys
really good singers
lots of hit records

I was a bit out of my element

I liked the money
and the guys in the band
and the
treatment we got

reflecting back

maybe the topless joint
would have been
a better choice

bouncing breasts
interesting smart women
making good money
nice funk jazz to play

choices are so challenging

each choice
can spin each life
around
we will never know

**SO**

can't know
a crap shoot
the choices we make

**very**

**random**

# New Shit

WHEN WE WROTE ON PAPER
OR A TYPEWRITER
STUFF DID NOT DISAPPEAR
OR MAKE LETTERS CAPITAL
WHEN WE WANTED THEM
LOWER CASE

THIS DIGITAL SHIT HAS
TOO MUCH A MIND
OF IT'S OWN
ALWAYS WANTING
TO MAKE THINGS RIGHT

NOT CONDUCIVE TO ART
WHICH IS ABOUT
MISTAKES AND DISCOVERY

TO MAKE A WRONG NOTE FIT
TO NOT START
EACH LINE WITH A BIG LETTER
TO MAKE MISTAKES RIGHT
AND RESOLVED

DON'T FUCKING CORRECT
MY SPELLING
IT MAKES IT HUMAN
AND MISS.LEADING

YOU ARE SUCH A
SMART BITCH
WHO NEEDS TO
FIX EVERY MISTAKE

EVERY DISCOVERY
WAS MADE BY
A WRONG TURN
A MISTAKEN
READING OF THE
MAN MADE COMPASS

OF WHAT IS RIGHT
AND WHAT IS WRONG
BEING
OFF COURSE

NOT FINDING
WHAT WE WERE
LOOKING FOR

FINDING SOMETHING
UNKNOWN

THE NEED TO BE ON COURSE
IS A BEAUTIFUL WAY
TO GET LOST

STEPHEN JAY GOLDBERG

**100**

# BLACK and **WHITES**

There is no greater sin than desire,

No greater curse than discontent,

No greater misfortune than wanting something
    for oneself.

Therefore he who knows that enough is enough
    will always have enough.

-Tao Te Ching 500 BC

## – one –

I DON'T FEEL SO GOOD TONIGHT. IT'S LIKE IT ALL FLASHES IN front of me and I haven't done a damn thing. I've been a fake, a fraud. The stupid thing is I haven't enjoyed most of it.

The facts are I'm forty-nine years old and played the role of an artist, a painter artist most of my life. Like I said, today was a bad day because I destroyed all my paintings, over two hundred of them. My wife is sleeping upstairs, I haven't told her yet. I mean they were all pretty much the same, black and white, four feet tall, eight feet wide, done with rollers, fast stroke stuff. I enjoy the aging of the paint on roller, the imperfections the roller develops as the paint, exposed to atmosphere, slowly dries, making tiny lumps in the nap, the inconsistencies and the variance of pressure as the paint is applied to the surface.

We live in the woods in upstate New York, two hours from the city. I made this big fire of them, the black and white four by eights.

The upsetting thing was, when I started the fire the dogs started to bark, so I threw them all the meat in the fridge to shut them up. Neeta is gonna be really pissed, I call her Neeta, her name is Anita. She buys this meat from this organic farm and watches the animals get slaughtered, she says if you can't deal with it, the slaughter, the death, don't eat it. We have chickens and she chops their little heads off, I mean I can't watch it. I don't really like chicken. She's really comfortable with death. When I ask her about it she says, "You live, you die, that's it." I don't really get it, it scares the hell out of me. I mean death.

I don't think about it when I'm doing my black and whites. But I also drink a bottle of Scotch and chain smoke Lucky Strikes while I'm doing them, vodka in the summer. I don't discuss this stuff with Neeta. I used to, and she'd say "Enjoy each day you have, make the most of it, you'll

STEPHEN JAY GOLDBERG

**102**

never have it again," it was always a good opportunity to make love, this today stuff. Making love, having sex, always had the ring of death to it, I mean for me. She has this gift, Neeta does, to accept things how they come, I didn't have that blessing. I mean I don't accept anything, coming or not coming.

I have one child, I almost said "kid," I hate that term "kid," it's like "wow." He's from a long gone girlfriend who died from an overdose of heroin. He happily found me when he was sixteen, his name is Sidney too. He had a really rough time, he's been a total joy to me, he's now twenty-four, he plays the saxophone. His mother was my first real love but she walked. We were sitting in Washington Square Park, she said, "Sid, you don't know how to love anyone but yourself." I tried to explain that the last person I loved was myself. We were taking all these pills, Ludes. I didn't know she was pregnant. She said, "I'm going to see my folks." When I asked her for her phone number she made up a number, there was no such area code. She was no older than twenty, more like seventeen. She was smart and beautiful, the first love. Dark thick hair, black eyes, so hot, the only word is bursting, bursting with life, she burst with life. We made love, expressed passion like we owned it, like no one else had ever done it before. I don't need to go into details, that's what poetry and music are for.

We had this little place on East 9th Street between Avenue A and Avenue B, where there was no food except rice, cheap rice and some vegetables. We would take these pills and hold each other. I got the news she was dead from an OD, heroin, from Bathsher, a friend who would chip in for food, rather than spend it in restaurants. He took care of Charlie Parker at the end of Bird's life and had all these great stories about Bird. This creep dealer, Andre, was always after Renee, he most likely OD'ed her so he could have sex with her almost dead, beautiful perfect body. And she was perfect, Renee, she was my first love and I understand how she liked heroin more than me. I really do understand that, I'm not that likable and drugs can be more friendly than people.

He calls me, the one who plays saxophone, mine and Renee's, he calls me Sidney, like me, that was Renee's idea. To call our son my name. No Jr. crap. We had a good laugh about it. Sidney and I still laugh about it. He's a good young man. The amazing thing is Neeta is into it, the boy. She has this gift, Neeta does, to accept things how they come, I didn't have that blessing. I mean I don't accept anything, coming or not coming.

# – two –

WHEN I BURNED THE DAMN THINGS, I COULDN'T BELIEVE THE smoke. My puny Lucky was nothing compared to the painting fire. The dawn coming up. The fire and smoke far more beautiful and interesting than the paintings. I don't know any smoke signal stuff or I would send one up. Neeta's up there sleeping.

Now there's a thing about sleeping women that drives me crazy, I could almost kill them. There they are dead, so I have to sneak around, tiptoe around, like sleep is this damn religion. Neeta is like that, hates to be woken up, I stay up all night, then sneak into bed, the comfortable bed, like a thief, don't breathe, don't move, don't move a sheet or a cover, so I drop the pills, pain killers, tranqs on top of the alcohol, and I look at her perfect face, perfect body, just there dead, gone. I smell her sweet breath and think, I made paintings, art, above and beyond, but not tonight, tonight all fire, all hungry dogs, I want to drive the car into walls and more walls. Yet I sneak into bed, into safety, rub against her, a little sound, a moan, an "I'm sleeping sound." The thing is her breath, even in sleep, it's so sweet. Not honey sweet, it's like her insides are good, human sweet. That never fails to impress me.

I feel all this power, physical power next to her and wait for the pills to kick in, like this mini death, a spinning mini death that I will never talk to her about, and she is the only one left to talk to. I've long ago lost any friends I had. She'll rise in the morning, all clear, all alive, and have a purpose to do things, to get on with it.

The sun comes in, I hear the shower running, toilet flushing, I feel myself drifting. The window is open, just a crack, I can smell the smoldering black and whites, it was hard to get them going, the fire in the field, I had a hard time finding the gas can, the one for the lawn mower. It was like this giant sandwich, like grilled cheese in the old toaster oven I used to have on the lower east side, that wouldn't shut itself off, the timer was screwed up and I'd burn everything, look in the little blackened window and see the smoke, it was before smoke alarms and seat belts and back up disks, like you screwed up too bad, no parachute.

God these pills feel great, mixed with the scent of smoldering black and whites, like this yin yang incense. I want to get up and eat, make this huge breakfast, it's the only meal I really like, the only one I really eat, I mean as a meal, it's sometimes the only reason to get up. We have chickens, like I said, I don't like eating them, the birds themselves, but I like the eggs, I always did like eggs.

I'm not thinking about Neeta's reaction to the fire, some of the paintings are probably half burned, they might look better. I keep thinking of the term "reductionist," like it's this new movement in the art world, make a piece and reduce it to it's most painful moment and cut out all the rest. I've been so careful, too careful. Four by eight masonite, painting it flat black, then drinking a bottle of whiskey, and putting a fast roller of white on it and pretending it was important, even eastern. The eastern thing was carrying the stuff out to burn, masonite is pretty heavy.

I don't know how's she's going to react to my fire. She could be totally cool about it and say it was the right thing at the right moment or want to kill me, that's the great thing, I never know what she might do. I mean in reaction to my acting out. She is pretty cool about her stuff. She takes care of the animals, dog, cat, and chickens. Then she plays the stock market on the computer for four or five hours, commodities or something that makes money, a lot of money. Sometimes when she's at it I get behind her and hold her beautiful breasts and say, "Support," she doesn't think it's that funny, then she can go out and kill a chicken and make really hot love with me, I can tell when she's hot because her lips get really swollen and even more beautiful. Then she gets back on the computer and it makes me really hot, I mean after twenty years it makes me really hot, like every time is the first time.

This morning is different because I've destroyed the black and whites.

Neeta doesn't eat breakfast, likes dinner, I never liked dinner. I want to kiss her, in her morning sleep, under these warm covers. "Comforter" is a good word. The pills and the alcohol seem like this anti-death stuff, yet in my mind I know it's the death stuff. Next to her I try to feel her youth and beauty going into me, like the cells of her body going into me. I tell myself how much I love her and kiss her back, soft, to not wake her. I remind myself how I need to do something good, and make all these promises to myself how I will do good for other people and know I will never do it. I need to sleep, and start over. Tomorrow I'll make everything better, I'll change it all, I can't sleep, the dawn is coming in. I'll take just two more pills, and start all over, better tomorrow.

# - three -

JESUS, IT'S TWO O'CLOCK IN THE AFTERNOON. WHAT THE HELL is that smell, like a fire, man oh man. Is that rain, that sound, or the radio between stations? My arm is stuck to the sheet, Jesus, it's blood. What the hell did I do to my arm. Mornings at best are confusing. Where is Neeta?

The note, taped up there to the mirror. I need some aspirin. Yeah, I keep them here next to the bed, water, I need some water. Water. It's here, spring water, I can taste the plastic, why do they put it in plastic, I don't get it. Spring water in plastic. Four aspirin, aspirin, to aspire to heights unknown. It creates a pleasant ringing in the ears. Everything hurts. Come on tough guy, come on phony, read it. One of those bold marker notes. Jesus, I'm still dressed. My glasses, where are they, screw glasses, I hate glasses, I think glasses kill old people, the unnatural weight on the nose and ears cut off the blood to the brain. I have a theory about sight, too complicated to go into. In my shoe, I put them in my shoe. Put the damn ugly things on. Here we go, the note. Jesus my knees hurt and the sheet is stuck to my arm. I like to see myself in the mirror without my glasses but I can't see myself clearly without my glasses.

The note: "Get out, just go, it is not interesting, it is not fun, I mean it, Sid, get out, now, today. I've had it. I put your stuff in the Subaru wagon, take it and go. There's a wallet on the seat, with some cash and a credit card with a five thousand dollar limit, just go, I can't take it any more. I agree with you, you don't have any talent. That's what you said when you got into bed and woke me up. I'll tell you the truth, when I saw the burnt paintings, I was thankful, relieved that it was over. And it is over. I'll be back here at three o'clock, to feed the chickens. Please if you ever had any feelings for me, please don't be here. And I know how many years it has been. Be kind for once in your life and JUST GO!

Anita."

Okay, okay, the keys, the keys, they must be in the car. Oh man, I feel bad. I can't get this sheet off my arm. I'll drive the wagon behind the barn and hide there. No screw that, I'll drive to Atlanta and hang with John for a few months and she'll miss me bad, and I'll have a party and paint five hundred new paintings. That's what I'll do. She can't take it, well I can't take it either. Bye bye birds, key birds. Bye bye Jesus, I did it, I really did it, I fired them up, burnt the fuckers. Good for me. They were crap, lies. I admit it. I'm no artist, I'm a phony. Okay, okay, okay.

What do I do? Who am I kidding? I can't drive, look at my hands, I'm shaking. Maybe they weren't too bad, the black and whites, they were bold, damn bold. They're gone, gone and thank God they are. Okay, okay, what, what, what do I do? Get this damn sheet off my arm. Nice little red splotch, a blood-sheet painting. A beer, yeah a beer and a few pills, no screw that, I'll flush them down the toilet, yeah, no I better not do that, I'll just take a few and a beer. Then I'll go to that Buddhist place. What the hell is the name of it, that place up past Albany, think man. I can't remember the name. The Sanda something, I can't remember. I'll go to a Holiday Inn for a few days, just to cool out, go in the pool, take a sauna, clean out. Yeah, take a notebook and a sketch pad and that book, *The Three Pillars of Zen*, where the hell is it. Yeah, the Holiday Zen. Okay three pills and a beer to stop shaking. I got to get out of here, for her, for me. Okay be clear, Sid, be clear!

Oh that tastes good, I don't even like beer, but it tastes good on the tongue, carbonation. I'll be okay. This is a breakthrough. Empty the cup so it can be filled. I don't need a thing. It's spring. I feel better. There's buds on the trees and I'm free. Look at that bird, that's amazing, just flying around. It's better, the beer and the pills kick in, so I'm off. How do they land on that thing? Amazing, they just come in at a hundred miles an hour and hit the little peg on the feeder. Take a little seed and off they go. Amazing!

I'll leave a little note. "Neeta babe, I love you. I'll come back in better shape, the paintings weren't that good, we both know that, so I'm out of here, thanks honey. I'll come back a new man. You made a good choice, telling me to go. A rut is a rut. Love you, Sid. You're hot." No cut the "You're hot" stuff. I mean she is hot, but yeah cut it. Yeah, it's cut, crossed out heavy, so she'll wonder what I crossed out. I have to make it dark, so she can't read it.

# - f●ur -

SHE LEFT THE KEY RIGHT IN THE IGNITION, LIKE SHE MUST
think I can't function at all, I'm fine, good. Off I go. A little turn of the
wheel and I'm dead, I'm almost dead anyway, but to die in this piece of
crap car, ugly car, like dying in a cheap tuna can. 87 north, it's just getting
dark, I want to go home, no the next Holiday Inn sign, I'm there, check
in. Turn it Sid, the wheel, bam and you're dead, save us all a lot of boring
trouble, just bam, off the interstate, into the side rail. It's dark, so damn
dark, I hate driving in the dark, all oncoming headlights. I'll get off right
after Albany. I'll hire a hooker, maybe two hookers, stop at a liquor store,
get some good bourbon, have a little fun, I have the damn credit card,
then I'll find the Buddhist place. Empty the cup before it can be filled.
I don't want to miss her. I want her to miss me, I'm sure she's glad I'm
gone. She's probably at the computer making money, doing the market.
Past Albany, maybe I'll go to Montreal. There's the sign, Holiday Inn, exit
ramp and I'm there. I hate this car, no power, I'll trade it in tomorrow for
one I like, something that moves.

    I don't know if I'm doing this or imagining it, dammit. I've been
through this before and each time it's more frightening, more terrible
and I go on and on, done it, done it! I am in the car, alone. When I'm
alone things are less and less real, I'll know I'm going to crash the car, I
know it, I can't drive, can't focus, Jesus, I'm going too slow, everything is
passing me. Hold on Sid, just hold on. Why am I such a coward, so afraid,
everything so unreal, so uncomfortable, like being alive doesn't quite fit,
it never fit, never. For as long as I can remember, it never fit, never felt
quite right, except sometimes with the drugs or the drink, but just for
a second, for a minute, then more torturous. God, I've got to hold this
wheel, hold on, hold the wheel and steer. But why, "why." For the others

Rants Raves & Ricochets

109

asshole, the ones that are okay, the ones that don't want to die. Not in a wreck, please God, not in a wreck.

That's how it happened, way back then, in a wreck. Mom and dad, an ugly wreck in dad's white Buick Convertible, those cool vent holes in the side of the hood. I don't know who they were. Coming home from their fun weekend in the mountains. Hitting a damn trailer truck head on. The top down at night. They thought they were damn movie stars, mom's red hair blowing in the wind, dad driving too fast. Cigar in his mouth. Me and Jason home in Queens with the maid, Cleo. Me eleven, him fourteen. Then the phone call. Cleo all freaked out. Dad died on the spot, it seemed like years till mom was well, she was never really well after that, always in pain and this confused look on her face. Our aunts, dad's sisters, took care of us, they'd take turns, always criticizing each other's housework. They were okay to Jason and I.

Where's the damn exit, where are you. A sign, "Next Exit 12 miles," I missed it. God dammit, I missed it. Twelve miles, I'll never make it. Jesus. Okay man cool out, you're gonna be okay. Don't do it, don't do it. Hold the damn wheel, look ahead, the road, the trees, the other cars. It's like I'm not moving and they're passing through me. No, I'm gonna be okay, make it to the motel, have a few drinks. I'm not gonna die on this interstate. How the hell did they build all this shit, all so perfect. What did I build, nothing, nothing, nothing. Some goddamn useless paintings. I could have painted these lane lines, these dotted lines, at least they would have had some purpose, and I could have gotten paid and come home tired every night. Or gone out for a beer with the other guys on the crew and complained how hot it was or how cold it was and done something honest for once in my life. It's too late for that now. All those damn nights and days, knowing it was a lie. The abstraction, it wasn't abstraction, it was excuses, bullshit. Why am I cursed with knowing that. Jesus, how do those guys drive those huge trailer trucks. They do it and get paid to do it, maybe that's sanity. Talking to each other on their CB radios, getting paid to bring things from here to there, drive a huge damn truck, like a goddamn man. Who cares what it is or what it means? Look at that son of a bitch go. He could wipe up us all out, go nuts and smash up everything on the highway, kill us all. He brings the stuff from here to there. All the crap that's devouring the human race. He's better than me. Better than I could ever be.

I don't know where I'm going, or why. To make some stupid marks on a canvas, or I should say masonite, I'm too damn cheap to paint on canvas. Neeta would say, "Sidney, paint on canvas like a real artist." Marks, roller strokes that no one cares about, that serve no function. Damn it, if I hit that guardrail I bounce off and hurt the ones that are okay, the salesmen, the schoolteachers, the guys who paint the lines. Hold it Sid, clear and steady. There it is, the exit. Turn the wheel. I made it.

Why did I have to be so afraid, back then, back there, a minute ago. Because I'm so close to losing it. A little turn of the wheel, inches, move the steering wheel six inches and I'm dead, that's not right, to think like that. Some screwed up wiring in the brain. If I would have been on some kind of medication forty years ago it all could have been different, but I was always too proud or dumb to admit the wiring screwup. I thought it made me "creative," what a joke. A joke on me. Thank God, I'm off the interstate. And no one knows or cares because I'm nothing, nobody. I annoy myself until I shut off the mind, the annoying brain. This head talk show that I don't ever want to hear. The damn station that's locked in. I wonder what the truckers say to each other on the CB's. Probably stuff like "The hash browns at Mary's Diner were greasy as hell" or "The cops are all out along I-89 today" but they have all these other words, code words, another language, a man's language to say male things. I'm sure they don't say, "My hands are sweating all over the steering wheel because I'm thinking about killing everyone on the road including myself, because my life is one meaningless piece of crap!" Maybe I should get one of those CB's, to learn how to be a man. My mind is girlish, feminine, all talk no action.

# - five -

IT'S A NICE ROOM, JESUS, I MADE IT, GOT HERE. I THOUGHT THE check-in guy would be freaked out when he saw me but he took the credit card and gave me my room key, 201. It's all here, TV, telephone, bathroom, everything I need, so simple. Sort of an imitation Monet on the wall. If I could have sold one of my paintings to a chain like this I'd feel better, a lot better, I mean thousands maybe millions of people would see it, wake up to it, fall asleep to it, have sex to it. I'm no good, no damn good. Maybe fifty people have seen my "work," my lies. Now this is a place I could kill myself in.

My old friend Mal's mother killed herself in a motel room, slit her wrists. We were in our twenties, Mal told me how they charged him for the mattress. Ruined from all his mother's blood. He took her to see the movie *The Birds*, after taking her out of the mental hospital. He thought a movie would be a good idea, someplace in Jersey. He told me about it, like he was talking about nothing, another movie, he ended the story with, "What a drag." He worked as an usher in a midtown movie house and was learning to play the trumpet. He had this nice little place on Carmine Street in the Village. He also told me an old Italian guy came up to his fourth-floor walkup with a gun and told him to shut up the damn horn. Mal gave him a little push and he fell down the stairs and died. Mal went back to his scales but never made it as a horn player.

I would do it in the tub, nice warm bath, a slit here and there, and goodbye. Empty the tub all nice and clean. This room is nice. Overlooks the parking lot, I can see the Subaru and the trees. And all the other cars, like sleeping death machines, so ugly, all of them. Men work in factories making those things, the cars, the parts, putting them together, getting paid, go home to wives and kids and they feel good, good and tired and honest. Go out and have a beer after work, shoot some pool, watch some football or basketball. Play with the kids on weekends, order pizza, and the rest of it. Even this building, this room, has meaning to the men who designed it, the men who built it. They can drive by fearlessly and say, I poured the cement, I did the electric, papered the seams on the wallboard. Had a part in building that. I have never had anything close to that feeling. I've wasted my life.

I need to go to a gun store. I've never shot a gun but one time is enough. It's four o'clock. My eyes hurt from staring at the road.

Guns, I look in the phone book, guns.

I've bought the gun, the place was not that far from the liquor store, the guy was a pretty nice guy, the guy at the gun store. I told him, I'm interested in target shooting, that I had been a great tennis player till my legs went and now, in my later years, I need something more exciting than darts. The woman at the liquor store was less friendly, I bought myself a half gallon bottle of their best vodka, Stoli. I always drink the cheap stuff but this is a big night. I didn't have much trouble driving because I ate all the pills I had left. Eight pain killers, codeine and five tranqs, Librium and two bourbons at the ugly bar. I hate bars in the daytime. It stunk from vacuum cleaner exhaust.

# - six -

I GO BACK TO THE CRUMMY HOTEL BAR AFTER A LITTLE disturbed nap. Night at last.

Somehow I've managed to pick up this woman at the bar, I've paid for her drinks, pushed the card, she's not very pretty and has this drunk grating laugh. I want to go back to my room and blow my brains out. She's into this conversation with the bartender about some people that I don't know. I push a twenty dollar bill her way, I'm thinking about the new gun I've bought and how bad she looks. How first I'll kill her and then me. She herself thinks she's sexy, she's a bar spent babe with dyed hair and sickening perfume. I tell her I'll give her fifty bucks to come back to my room. Yeah, I'll tell her I'm a famous artist, headed into the city to see my agent and I feel like doing some drawings of her, I'll ask her if she's ever modeled, yeah, I'll tell her she looks like a model, if she ever stops talking to the damn bartender. What is the deal with bartenders? I was gonna go to bartender school about a hundred years ago.

A mixologist, I even went up to the place in Flushing, Queens, the Flushing School of Mixology. The guy who ran the place showed me the little book on mixed drinks and there was this little bar set up in the second-floor walkup. It gave me the creeps. It was real for about ten seconds, then I bagged the whole thing, like I bagged everything else. I bagged every good decent idea I ever had and did or non-did the things between the ideas the non-things, by some miracle I survived. Till now. It's a joke, a real bad joke. Finally this creep bartender in this place has to go make some mixology. I don't know if I can talk. I still try, beaten to the ground and I still try. Humans are amazing, hooked and reeled into hopelessness and we still go on and on. One more shot, even after the game is over with, keep going at all costs, keep going. As if the mouth isn't bleeding or the heart isn't broken. Just keep going.

She says, "Yeah I use to do some modeling." Yeah like for the horse show.

"I can tell, something about the way you carry yourself." Somehow, I speak. She hasn't gotten off the bar stool.

"Maybe we could do it tomorrow."

"That would be great but I have to be in the city by noon, meeting my agent for lunch."

Why am I doing this, to save myself for a few more hours. Screw it. Amazing how the preservation part of the mind keeps going, keeps working.

"I could use a few more sketches for the show."

"You mean tonight?"

"That's all there is, tonight. I'm out of here first thing in the morning, I'm on my way back from Montreal. I mean I could pay you. And they'd be in an art show in New York, my sketches of you. You have a quality I'd like to draw. They may even develop into paintings. I mean it's up to you."

"You mean like studies?"

"Yeah, you could call them that."

"I don't know."

"Why don't we have another drink and we can think and talk about it."

"You have art supplies with you?"

"Pen and ink, no turning back, I mean with ink. You make a line and it's there for good, it's history."

"Are you famous?"

"There aren't any famous artists anymore, not like before TV or movies, ninety-nine percent of the population couldn't name a living artist if they tried, but they can name any second-rate actor on any network sitcom."

Jesus that was good, the mind is amazing.

"You know you're right. I know Picasso and Van Gogh and that might be it. But are you famous?"

"In my world, the art world, yes."

"Well that's good."

"It's the same with composers, do you know the name of one living serious music composer?"

"No, you're right. I know Bach and Beethoven."

"And that's it."

"Yeah, that's it, and Brahms."

"The three B's."

"Yeah, the three B's. So do I have to pose nude?"

Jesus, what am I doing, I can't believe I can talk. She's going for it. Should I tell her how stoned I am, that I have a gun in my room, that I'm going to put a bullet through my head and hers if she comes back with me. Her bullet could go through her stomach; I would never shoot through a woman's breast or brain. I've never even shot a gun. I tell the creep bartender double bourbon and a Manhattan for the lady, she says in honor of my show. She looks about fifty, who's trying to look thirty, died black hair, nice full body, sad dark eyes, wearing a black low cut dress with a faded jean jacket, she has that sort of greasy face that gets creamed every night, God I wish I didn't eat all the pills in the car, the can, the Subaru tuna can of death. She still hasn't gotten off the bar stool, who cares, tall, short, one legged, who cares.

"Yeah, well I can pose for a few minutes, after our drinks."

I want to say no, forget it, it's too late, I'm going back to my room to blow my brains out, you'll see it in the morning papers, you'll be famous, you'll tell the TV cameras how you talked to me in the bar and how I seemed depressed, then you went to the parking lot and heard the shot but figured it was just another blow out. But no.

I can't find the key, the last double was too much, she goes through my pockets, gets the key and opens the door. Inside:

"So you're an artist!"

She slams me to the floor.

"Come on artist! Produce! You think my life has been a bowl of cherries. Look!"

She takes off her jacket, then fast, off goes the dress, bra, stockings, panties, pulls off all her clothes, everything, and she's scarred, badly scarred, her breasts, her stomach, her back, terrible deep scars. She looks like her skin is made of those cheap bamboo blinds.

"A fire, you bastard, you want to paint this, you want to draw this, two kids dead, burnt in the fire. I was drunk and went for a walk, to get another bottle. When I got back I ran into the blaze and woke up in the hospital a week later. That would make a painting, me on fire, burning up. Mister Cool, you want to take that to your fucking gallery, woman on fire, draw me, make a study of this!"

She puts on her black pointed high heels.

"You think you suffer, let's see, let's see your scars."

She kicks me in the head, then the gut, then the balls.

"Let's see, big shot."

"There's a gun in the dresser, use it, bitch, use it!"

STEPHEN JAY GOLDBERG

"No, you're gonna make love to me, like you wanted to, no art, no bullshit, come on, come on."

She's burnt, the woman, like my black and whites.

"Come on big man."

I feel the blood running down my face. She undoes my pants and pulls them down around my ankles. She's standing over me. My thought is, I'm gonna have to pay for the carpet if I bleed all over it. I tell her, "The bed, let's get on the bed!"

"NO! No, no, no, you bastard. Smart ass bastard."

God how I deserve this, she's right.

"I'm fifty years old, look at this, look what I did to myself, for being stupid, not paying attention. I don't even know how it happened."

She takes the pillowcase off the pillow and wraps it around my head.

"It's nothing, a scratch, you bleed on the carpet you'll have to pay for it. My name is Audrey Beckett, like Beckett the writer, Samuel Beckett, my favorite is "Malone Dies," not the plays, read the novels. Stop bleeding, okay, what's your name."

"Sid."

"Full name."

"Sid Green."

"Yeah you look kind of green, I like Jews, always so troubled."

She's still standing over me, straddling my bleeding head. The scars stop at her upper thighs, between her knees and her opening, all parallel. I feel a drop from her opening, it drops into my eye. She puts her foot on my mouth.

"Now, live or die!"

I see all these things in my eyesight, moving things, filled with life, microbes, her microbes, little fast-moving lines, like on a film when the movie is over.

"I swear I'll crush the life right out of you."

"Die."

She walks away and sits on the bed, the bed cover.

"I have no nipples, they were burnt off in the fire, do you see that?"

"Yes, I'm sorry, you're still attractive."

"It's not your fault, it's my fault, for not paying attention."

The moment is so sober, so frightening. Her black eyes look into me so hard. I crawl up between her legs, the part that is unburned.

"I'm sorry, stay and let's go to sleep."

She slams her knees into my ears, again, and again and all there is is ringing, bells, the bells of Saint Audrey, her thighs open and close like those things on crabs, those little shutters or a machine in a steel factory.

The softness is around my head and she squeezes hard, hard, hard. A something, a knee in my face and she's gone. She dresses in a blur and is gone. The door opened and closed. Dots of blood on the blue carpet like some colorful oriental language. She took my pants, stole my wallet. No there they are. That's my mind, not hers. I search through the pockets and yes, three pills broken into pieces, I swallow and find a full pack of cigarettes in my jacket.

I light one and switch on the TV. I can't see it, I'm crying, catch my breath, wipe my eyes, focus God damn it! It's Letterman talking to some perfect babe about her latest movie, blond hair, black tight top, no burns. She says, we had a lot of fun on location in Hawaii. They show a clip, it's this babe in a bikini on a speed boat shooting an automatic gun at the speed boat following her, choppers flying overhead, her breasts all bouncing, just almost bouncing out with the firing automatic, the music all in sync. The clip ends. The audience applauds, a blockbuster. I go to the dresser and get out the handgun and hold on to it for dear life. Warm it between my thighs, the nozzle pointed up. Now if she comes back on, the babe, Saint Audrey of the Flames, I'll blow her away, like Elvis did, shoot the bastards, call room service and order a few more TV sets, blow them all away, then start on the radio, there is no radio.

# - seven -

I REMEMBER BEING A LITTLE KID ALONE IN A MIAMI HOTEL room. With a pile of quarters to put in the slot on the radio. My parents probably getting stoned at the hotel bar. I used to like to look in the back of the radio and see the bright lights in the vacuum tubes. I imagined they were little tiny brightly lit stages with microscopic performers, little Charlie McCarthy and Edgar Bergen, Amos and Andy, Burns and Allen, Jack Benny, Nick Carter, in these bright points of light.

The mornings back in Queens, mom smoking her Chesterfields, listening to Arthur Godfrey talking in this nice throaty voice introducing Julius LaRosa and the rest of his little gang, something sinister about him. Little did I know what I was in for.

When mom died, I was the only one left, in my late twenties. Jason never got back from Korea. I had to pick out mom's coffin, after I sold her diamond ring to pay for the funeral. A whole basement filled with coffins. I picked one of the cheapest ones. Then I had this bad dream about having to go back every day and putting a quarter in the push slot, like on an old pinball machine, like the pay radio. So I bought the cheapest coffin. I figured the worms would get through quicker. They had some that were impenetrable, stupid. I told the guy, the funeral director, he seemed like the same guy from mixology school. I told him I wanted an open coffin. But when I came back the next night I took a look at her I told them to close it. I didn't dare touch it. They had put this lacy thing in her hair, really bad, but I didn't have the nerve to take it off her, to touch her, she looked too weird, the makeup and stuff was ridiculous. Like let's make her look like Ann Margaret. I wanted to laugh and cry at the same time. I knew she wasn't in there, in the box or in the body and it was good it didn't look like her. Dad, years before looked a lot better. The whole death thing is creepy. I should leave a letter letting them know what to do with me. Like put me in a paper shredder and use me to chum for sharks, something impossible, like death is as impossible as life is.

Okay, right here and now I've got to make a choice. This gun feels so good to hold. An amazing machine. It should be X-rated to show a gun. In fact the word "Gun" should be X-rated. Cross out "Fuck" and put in "Gun." Now I put the thing in my mouth, no against my temple. Where's the damn remote, shut up! Another hip black comedian making jokes about race crap. Got it. Off! Thank God. The choice is, put this babe against my temple and squeeze, or....or what. Go to sleep and head for the Buddhist place in the morning or go back to the bar. No it's closed, or get in the car and drive, foot down, no, I might kill innocent people.

Like I killed my father. He would say, "Sidney, you're killing me with your behavior." Then he died, a few months later. Leukemia. My mother looked at me and said, "I loved that man more than I could ever love you. Are you happy? Look what you did." She did, she really said that. Just because I went to the Lower East Side and bought high rise double saddle stitched pegged pants and put Pomitex on my hair. He said "You look like a Spick. This is a reflection on your parents." Now I thought I looked cool and so did the girls and he thought it was to hurt him. Dad, I was only trying to get girls. I thought it really wasn't fair that they got to sleep together and I had to lay in bed alone. I mean at twelve or thirteen, I am goddamn alone. Look at this crummy motel, I Am God Damn Alone!

The choice is, blow my brains out or find the Buddhist place and cool out, find fucking God, peace. Got it, got it, got it! Take the gun to the Buddhist place and give it three days, if I'm not okay, find the thing, the comfort, nirvana, the reality. Kill all of them, then myself. Say, Mister B-men, you have three days and three nights to clear this shit up then it's over. One way or another. No fucking ten years in lotus and kissing Buddha's ass and staring at a wall. No years of chanting and getting buzzed on the vibrations of gongs. You see boys, I've got a piece of machinery that's "now," realization on demand, an enlightenment holdup. If that isn't Zen, what is? That's the deal. But if I wake up and would rather die than make the walk to the bathroom to piss that's okay too. How the hell am I ever going to sleep? But I do, it fades and drifts into nothing.

I wake dressed on the bed, under the bedspread. The gun and the remote snuggled together on the night table, a wonderful couple. I pick up the phone.

"Room service, a pot of coffee, a bottle of aspirin, bacon and scrambled eggs, home fries, a double order of rye toast, a Remy Martin, a double

Remy and if you could, a pack of Pall Malls. Put it on my card. No I don't want a paper."

Jesus, I've got to change it all, it's not too late for me. God my head hurts. One word comes, it's "Selfless." Yeah, I know that last night should have been a lesson. Do something for other people, stop being so damn needy. The Buddhist place, grow some vegetables, clean up the mess, start here, now, in this room. I'm okay, I really am. But what's the name of the place. Shit, I can't remember it. The phone book, the yellow pages. A Buddhist retreat is not gonna advertise. I can't drive, I'm too shaky. Jesus, there's the gun, it smells, like it was fired. I'm not shot, the burnt woman! Shit, the phony Monet. I shot the phony Monet. Look at that, right through the iris. Not bad. If I could just go home for a few days and get it together. I'll call Neeta and ask her. No, no, no good. I'll go back when I have it together. Who am I kidding? The truth is, I don't know what to do. A knock on the door.

"Room service."

"Yeah, come in."

I'll give the guy five bucks, selfless.

"Here you go, thanks."

"Thank you sir."

"Yeah, put it down. What's your name?"

"Bob."

"Well Bob, can I ask you something?"

"Sure."

"How do you like your job?"

"It's okay."

"I never had a job, I just bullshit people. I thought I was an artist but I'm not. I don't know what to do. What should I do?"

"You need to sign the check."

"Bob, how old are you?"

"Twenty-two."

"What are you going to do with your life?"

"I'm going to pre-med, to be a doctor, a surgeon."

"Your parents must be proud."

"They're dead, cancer, I want to cure it."

"That's a wonderful thing son. My parents are dead too."

"Well, you enjoy your breakfast sir."

"What would you do, I mean if you were my age and had no future."

"I think I would go to some south sea island and fish and maybe write books or poems and study nature. Find a young native wife. I wouldn't eat bacon or eggs or drink coffee or alcohol or smoke. I'd try to live a simple life and at night I'd study the sky or maybe just look at it, lying on the beach or walking in the warm salt water and listen to the tree frogs and the waves. Maybe read all the classics in the sunlight, without rushing through them. Or maybe just be."

"That's pretty good Bob, thanks."

"Thank you. You enjoy your breakfast and the day."

"Hey Bob, are you going to do that, when you get old?"

"I don't know, people change. You should eat your breakfast before it gets cold."

"You want to join me?"

"I have to get back to work, to pay for school. Cancer, I'm going to fix it, thanks anyway."

"Good luck, Bob. And Bob, what do you mean, just be?"

"Well I have a cassette machine in my car and I play this new age stuff on my way to work, after school, and two days ago it stopped, stopped working, you want to hear this?"

"Yeah, I do."

"So then there's nothing, except I notice the sound of the tires on the road and the engine and cars passing and I notice there are people driving the cars, people who I don't know. So I noticed that was when my conscious brain cut in. So I try to cut off the brain cutting in and I can't, you know, the part of the brain that tells me what I'm doing. You really want to hear this?"

"Yes Bob, I really do."

"So it hits me, I'm not really there for any of it, everything has been this, being there to get someplace else. The day before we were cutting up cadavers and it was study, looking at the pieces. So...you want to hear this?"

"I want to hear this, yes."

"So there's a rest stop between school and here and I pull in and I get it. I mean it took a minute or two, looking out at the valley and Albany off in the distance. I get that we're brought up with and schooled with an analytical way of looking at things, this is this, that is that. But sir, that has nothing to do with reality, nothing at all. That was and is the best moment of my life, so far. Sir, your breakfast is getting cold."

"Bob, what could be a better moment?"

"I think falling in love, having children, procreating."

"Bob, you are going to be a great doctor. I'm going to wait for you to be my doctor, when I'm about to die."

"Sir"

"Sidney"

STEPHEN JAY GOLDBERG

"I have to get back to work."

"You're a smart kid."

"I'm learning."

"Bob, I want to ask you one thing. When you were cutting up the bodies, the cadavers, did you see yourself there, one of the dead ones?"

"Yes, I did, I thought, that is a human body and I am a human body, there was even a specimen about my age that was killed, or terminated in an automobile accident, he even looked a bit like me. We wanted to use his organs for transplants, but we couldn't get permission, everything about him was so young and vital but no family member would let us do it, it was a huge waste. The family said they wanted to bury him intact, for religious reasons. The very next day we watched a ten-year-old girl die who could have been saved by his liver. It's the way it goes."

"So where are you, in the rest stop getting it, or pissed at humanity?"

"In between, I'm learning, but I'm going to cure cancer I promise you that. I've got to get back to work."

"Good luck Bob."

"Thank you, sir."

# — eight —

I'M SO HUNGRY, IT ALL TASTES SO GOOD, THE EGGS AND BACON, the potatoes are a bit cold, and they're french fries, I thought I asked for home fries, always something wrong, they never get it all right. If I were a king or a god someone could die for that, cold potatoes, but I have no power except what I can pay for, the money, the twenty-three bucks for breakfast, and no one really gives a damn.

I open the curtains and look out on the parking lot. These cars looking into no place, one after another, sitting there with idiotic names, all so new, seventy cars worth twenty-thousand each, sitting there, a million and a half dollars worth of crap, sitting there, taking people places they didn't want to go in the first place and my stupid car there among them, staring off into space. How can I burn them all up, all at the same time. I take some of the cream that's for my coffee and use it to cover up the blood spots on the carpet.

As I pass by the front desk there are these Indian people, five or six of them, checking in. They're dressed in white robes and saris. There's an old guy with long white hair and a beard, he has this beatific half smile on his face. I go right up to him and ask him if he knows where the Buddhist retreat is. He has these piercing black eyes that seem to look right through me, I feel like he knows everything that's happened, he just says, "South," the single word "South." It makes me feel naked, the word, south. It keeps ringing in my head. The beautiful Indian woman says to me, "Swami G has just lead a retreat at the ashram, you missed it. It is twenty miles west of exit 14 of the highway. Ashram of the Hidden Light, you look like it will do you much good." She has this singing staccato accent. I just hang there, next to them, like I'm part of their group. The old guy puts this smooth black stone in my hand and smiles. It feels warm and smooth. I hold it and have this urge to cry, I feel it swelling in my throat, the sadness. Then they're gone. Like a cut in a movie or a dream. I look at the stone, it fits perfectly in my palm. It has this safety to it. It has a white vein going through it, not unlike one of my black and whites.

In the parking lot everything is horribly bright and clear, full sunlight, blue sky. Everything too well defined, stone in my hand. I don't have sunglasses. The tuna-can starts right up. I put the stone on the passenger seat, I almost want to seat belt it in, like a little frog. I think of Swami G getting the room I stayed in, and the coffee cream drying up to expose the blood stains and him studying the stains, the configuration of them, and the bullet hole in the Monet imitation and having some instrument of measurement, making perfect sense of them, like a score from some unplayed piece of music.

I have the gun in my pocket, I call it a "rod," I mean in my own mind. I figure I'm not a good candidate to "pack a rod." Or to "pack heat." I see what must be the guru's gray Mercedes. I want to leave the rod on his seat but the windows are locked even though the plate reads "Open." I toss it in the woods surrounding the parking lot. I am frightened and feel safe at the same time. Like this never-ending flood of thoughts keeps shooting through me. Every time I start to analyze events, to understand, to make sense of things, this shut up thing happens, like the anti-brain says, cut it man. The definition of the passing scenery gets more and more well defined. Clearer than clear. I have this horrible thought, like the stone has this chemical on it, like acid, that has gotten in through the pores of my skin, that is forcing me to experience the truth, or the horror of the truth, not just about me, but about existence. At one moment I'm saying, come on baby lets see it, then, cut it, no more. Then a third voice says, you're wasting time, you're driving yourself nuts, if you didn't get it by now you'll never get it. I pull the tuna-can out. God, how I hate driving. I drive for what seems like forever, have a few hits of what's left of the vodka and pull into a rest stop.

In the men's room, in the mirror, I don't know myself, completely unfamiliar. The stone is in my right-hand pants pocket. Washing my face doesn't help.

I lay down on what will be grass. Blue, blue, blue sky, I let my eyes close. I see Neeta behind my lids. Then this sniffing, this tickling sniffing and I'm looking into the eyes of a white poodle.

"She likes you. She doesn't bite."

I see these black heels sinking into the mud, a down elevator.

"Her name is Gita, give her a pet, she likes you. The truth is I'm too drunk to drive and it's only afternoon, but Gita had to pee and so do I. Now she might pee on you. You okay with that?"

From the angle that I'm looking this is Marilyn Monroe, all bursting and hot, like all her clothes are too small for her flesh.

"You coming from Albany?"

"I don't know."

"You headed for New York?" Now why is this babe talking to me.

"No, I'm going to a Buddhist retreat, to find myself."

"Well, I'm coming from this topless club in Albany, I was dancing there and they ripped me off. I got the flu, I mean I'm over it now. Can you imagine those bastards, they wouldn't pay me, it was six nights and I missed two, bastards. You like dogs? I lost my damn credit card and I need gas. I need some gas. You look pretty prone, I mean lying there. If I'm bothering you tell me." I ask her what she's driving.

"An eighty BMW, it's sweet."

Now I'm lying on the not grown grass, this poodle licking my face. She is the Buddha. Not the dog, the woman. I mean she's all back lit by the sunlight. I ask her if it's after five, she says it's four.

"I've got a deal for you, I say. We go to the next exit, we find a used car dealer, I sell my Tuna-Subaru for the first offer. We split the money and you drive me to New York." I mean I'm still prone on the grass. The poodle dog keeps on licking me. What could be more Zen? "Leather," she says, "the interior is leather, comfortable but it has a scent." She asks if I can get up. "Yes absolutely, I say."

Now a hand is a hand, but she helps me up and her hand is strong and warm and smooth. I ask her and me the same question. Why me? "Because you're here," she says.

She manages to follow me to the next exit, she's all over the road, we're going about ten miles an hour, cars zipping by, screw them, but no cops. We go to the first used car lot I see, Big Dads or some kind of shit. His first offer is six hundred bucks, I take it and tell him cash. I hand her three, and off we go. Me at the helm, the poodle on her lap. I still don't see her very clearly, it's like the sun is always behind her, but she has this movie star kind of thing, that interesting kind of voice that is more comfortable screaming than talking. Her outfit is this white, perfectly clean, one piece silk-like dress thing, when she turns it's like I can define her nipples more than her face. The sun does a great job on her nipples. Like Marilyn Monroe.

The strange thing, after we sell the tuna-can, is she's talking all this spiritual stuff, chain-smoking Lucky Strikes, which we both chain smoke. She goes on and on, chain talking, telling me the most wonderful life story, like a novel, but better because of her voice. All this stuff about countries I never heard of and being a young prostitute in Amsterdam. The whole time this little dog sort of freaking out, jumping from her lap to the back seat then onto my lap then back to her lap. I mean she gives me the most beautiful life history I've ever heard, with this little white dog freaking out all over the BMW. Like animated happiness.

Then she says to pull into the Motel on the Mountain, just as it's getting dark. I still can't see her, not clearly. She says she can't ride in a car in the dark. She says it's not night blindness, but the oncoming headlights that drive her nuts. The cool thing is everything she says makes me laugh, like the phrase oncoming headlights, it cracks me up. Like there's this irony in the phrase on coming headlights. And every time she cracks me up, she enjoys it more. So I'm thinking goodness is coming my way. I mean Neeta and I almost never laughed, or better yet, never laughed. Then she says, "STOP! Get out of the car, go, get out." While I'm laughing, she says "Go, get out." This place, The Motel on the Mountain, has this big uphill driveway. I stop the Beemer, she's all upset and she says, "Get out, GO! I'm sick of you." Now I think I'm pretty charming, so I ask her "Do you know who I am?" And she says, "Do you know who am? I'm a fucking movie star and I don't need you to hang on to me. Now get out! GO! I'm not kidding." I slam on the brakes, pull the E brake and get out.

So there I am again. It's like my life is this huge pile of books that I start to read but can never get past the first page. Like this guy I knew who was this big jazz fan, he'd get me over to his apartment, make me a drink and then say; "You've got to hear this piano solo, or this saxophone solo," record after record, like little pieces of things. After he'd find one, he'd be looking for another one, getting all hyper and sweating. He'd never play a whole record or even a whole tune until the whole place was covered with records and album covers, he'd be chain-smoking, there'd be ashes all over everything, he'd have four or five cigarettes going in different ash trays and keep pouring drinks in new glasses, he'd say stuff like, "Listen to what Bird played here." He'd be looking for certain phrases, all out of context, all screwed up, the records all skipped from him dropping the needle on them. Looking for that perfect sound, that perfect phrase that would blow me away. But they were all so disjointed, out of context, that they made no sense as isolated things, out of their environment. I'd say; "Leo, I've got to go," but he'd say, "Just check out this Trane solo, you got to hear how he did this" and he'd pour me another drink and on and on, till it was a blur. It would only stop when he ran out of cigarettes. I'd walk down Hudson Street, then Houston Street, the sun coming up, my ears ringing. I think Leo should have a thousand turntables and play all his records at once. I'd see him months later, he'd ask if I wanted to come up for a drink, I'd say, sure Leo.

Standing on the hill going up to the Motel on the Mountain, I don't even try to understand why Leo the jazz lover appears. Except for the out of context thing.

The stars are all out, bright as hell. So here I am, on this hill-driveway, the Motel on the Mountain. I really don't know which way to go. Down being easier, up being closer but harder. Or I could just pass out here. Fall into the woods and look at the stars, get sucked up by the stars. Like this sky power pulls me into an eternal life. I've dreamt about that shit, being pulled up into the sky, fast and clean. All this burning white. Pure, clean, clear.

And there they are, the oncoming headlights. I'm a deer about to be shot. The headlights stop. She says, "Get in." Down the hill, up the hill. "I wasn't really fair." She says, "I just lost a big contract for a big movie. So I took it out on you. I'm sorry. Get in, I've sent down for dinner, for both of us." Now I don't want to "Get in" but the decision is too quick to make, so I do get in. The Beemer is headed downward, to get up the hill you have to go down. The really bad thing is before she can make a U-turn, it's like forever, five or ten miles and we don't say a word. Then up the hill. Down the hill, up the hill.

She tells me her name is Laura Dean, now this is in yet another hotel bar. She says she's James Dean's kid and the greatest talent the world will see. I get out, manage to say, "What aspect of talent." She says, "Every aspect. Acting, writing, painting, composing, driving, directing, the whole deal, Sidney you've met your maker, this is your lucky night. You're a little old and ugly for me, but you need a change in the road. Am I right?" Now I see her, in the bar light. She has that look. Certain women have that look. Children of stars, aging women of stars. Who have had the money, the cool decadence, the body fixes. And the drugs of confusion.

Well let me tell you, Laura is the best. She cried and cried, I mean intimacy is something to cry about. She held the remote in her hand, looking for one of her movies or one of her dad's movies. She said, "How come they never show *East of Eden* on TV?" "Too good," I say. Now Laura is sucking up all this blow. She has it between her breasts on this nice part of her, like on her innocent breastbone. In this ritual like jar, like something you'd keep Sr. Dean's ashes in. It's the blue glass kind of deal.

She asks me, "Sidney, what's the deal, what's the deal. What are you looking for? I am so fucking down all the time."

She turns, Laura does. And there it is, this backbone and this ass and legs and feet. I reach over her and my hand hits the blow vial, between her nipples, like on my wrist. I take the blow vial, she mumbles, "Don't finish it, please Sidney." I snort a bit.

Now at this moment, I have never felt so much peace. The TV is on, the sound is off. The images move, and every image has hundreds of meanings, the hotel comforter is the perfect comfort, regardless how many others it made feel safe, who cares. God, how much I want the truth. As long as no one is excluded. I have the pain of greatness but not the luck or the timing. I even have the look of greatness. Laura is asleep or possibly dead, her body feels warm and safe. She is so troubled and has this sweet scent, except for her hair, which is all chemical. All this misguided shit. Mind going faster than understanding. In this bed I don't get what my body is, all this stuff built for us to fit in, in proportion. It was like when we had sex there was this truth and emotion, undeserving of any reality. She looks so sweet sleeping. God, how much I want to go home. But I know there's no turning back. I'm all confused. I can't sleep.

# - nine -

I GO THROUGH LAURA'S POCKETS AND FIND THE CAR KEYS. I
take the blow or what's left of it and hit the road in her car. I want to go
home. The Beemer has this nice leather smell to it. She has all these jazz
tapes. Down the hill, I find the interstate. North, man, north, home. This
car is so cool, no tuna-can here, the speedometer goes up to 160. I'm at
a hundred. We are hugging the road. There are the spinning lights. Just
appeared. So I crank it, I have this big band tape on really loud, Stan
Kenton or something, I see them in the rearview mirror, just fading away,
then gone, I'm doing a hundred and twenty, this baby is smooth, caviar.
Then, bam! Another patrol car coming down the ramp just ahead of me,
their spinners make it hard to see. Shit! I manage to get around them, the
Kenton brass screaming, Maynard the high note man, blowing his ass off.
Their stupid flashing lights fade like a Fourth of July sparkler, those idiots
could have killed me. I figure I better finish the blow in case those jerks
catch me. It's in one of those dumb designer vials, with the little spoon on
a little silver chain, I hate that crap. I slow down a bit so I can steer with
my elbow. The Kenton band is into a nice ballad. I snort up the stuff and
toss the cute little tinted bottle out the window. That thick brass sound
is embracing. This thing is a super HiFi with wheels. Then there they
are, the whole damn road blocked, three patrol cars. Screw them. Yeah
SCREW THEM! Then this white light and this beautiful huge crash, just
as the ballad ends.

The voice is saying, "Sir, get in the ambulance." I feel some warm
blood running down my face and into my mouth, it has a sweet taste to
it. There's a pain in my forearm. These guys look so serious, so heroic, so
together, a bunch of uniformed kids. The cops, the ambulance guys, all
clean-cut young kids. They look like newborn babies. I'm telling them I'm
okay. Again, "Sir, you need to get in the ambulance." They help me up and
off we go.

# - ten -

A GUY IN WHITE ASKS ME IF I'VE BEEN DRINKING, I TELL HIM, "Yeah, for about forty years." He says, "Well maybe it's time to stop." Then the ER. They put some kind of drops in my eyes and with a little tweezer pick the glass pieces out. They're all being so nice. I feel kind of okay, this nice-looking nurse gives me a shot. I ask her what happened. She tells me I have a broken arm and some stitches in my head and glass splinters in my eyes. I tell her I'm seeing okay and that she's a nice looking girl. I ask her if she'd like to lie down with me. She says no thank you and gives me some water through a straw. I drift off into this beatific sleep, where dreams are all vivid and white. Dreaming the nurse babe gets in next to me and there's this string quartet, all formal and all, it's the hotel Guru playing cello, they're playing this twelve tone stuff. We're on a plane, then on the back of this giant eagle-like bird. We set down on this clear water as I sink down all warm and safe. The nurse who is Laura is doing a sort of ballet over me and over her is the quartet on my black and whites, like big floats, big flotation sheets. Everything translucent, over the whole thing is a clear blue sky with these random birds passing over. The birds emit this sky writing kind of stuff, making more and more translucent levels of my black and whites.

"Breakfast Mr. Green, up and at 'em. Breakfast." Now this black nurse who looks sort of like Oprah is sitting me up. "You white people sure look ugly in the morning. Time to eat. Here baby, wipe your face." She hands me a washcloth, my right arm is in a cast and everything hurts, from top to bottom, mostly my head. "Somebody here to talk to you. Here's your breakfast, you need help, just ask."

"Hello Mr. Green, I'm detective Freed. Do you know you almost killed a police officer last night, go on eat your breakfast."

"No I didn't know that."

"Do you know you stole and destroyed a very expensive car."

"I think I do."

"Do you know you're going to jail. Do you remember having your rights read to you."

"No."

"Do you have a lawyer."

"No."

"Do you want a court appointed lawyer."

"Listen pal, I don't feel too good, so why don't you get the fuck out of here."

"Mr. Green you're in trouble, serious trouble. Do you know how fast you were going."

"I don't want to talk to anyone, mostly you, without a lawyer. I'll get my own lawyer, fuck face."

"Fine. When you get released from here, I'll see you in jail." And out he goes.

Oprah says, "Looks like you've been a bad boy."

"Yeah for an old guy I'm doing okay."

"There's a woman here to see you."

Now I'm thinking it's Neeta, who I really don't want to see. But no, it's Laura. At first I don't recognize her. She has on these shades and white fur coat, tight faded jeans and cowboy boots. Her blond hair all flowing.

"Sid, that was a bad idea."

"Sorry, it seemed like a good idea last night. So you like the Kenton band."

"Yes Sidney, my dad use to play trombone with him."

"No shit."

"Yeah, no shit."

"That's fantastic."

"He killed himself, so that wasn't so fantastic."

"I'm sorry. I hope the tape didn't get screwed up."

"No, the car's destroyed but the tape's okay. What about you, are you okay."

"Yeah, want to sign my cast?"

"I don't think so. Was I really such a bitch?"

"I don't know, I don't remember."

"I don't either. You shouldn't have taken my car."

Now she sits down on the bed next to me and takes off her shades. Her eyes look all blue and bloodshot, like she's been crying. She puts her hand on my leg and looks into my eyes.

"Sidney, I have insurance that will cover the car, I'll get something new, I'm thinking Porsche or Land Rover, I'm not sure."

"I'd go small and fast."

"Yeah I know you would. I'm not mad, I do that to people, that thing that pushes them over. You're not the first one."

"I thought your dad was James Dean."

"I lie all the time. Mostly when I do blow but it seems true at the time. Like the truth is an honest creative invention. I can't really figure it out."

"Me either."

"My dad really did play trombone with the Kenton band. That makes him pretty good, right?"

"Laura, that makes him really good."

"I'm not gonna press charges, I hate those pricks. Did we make love?"

"I don't remember."

"Neither do I. Listen Sid, I don't want this to get into the papers. Me and you and the car. So I'm going to get my lawyer to clean this up, fast and quick. That okay with you?"

"It's great, yeah, thank you."

"How's your arm."

"Cast in the part of a broken arm. Will you lay down next to me?"

"Sure, for a minute. Did you finish the blow?"

"Yeah I did, and tossed it."

"One less thing to worry about."

Now she falls asleep right here in the hospital bed next to me. In her fur coat, her over the covers, me under the covers. Her head on my cast, I sneak a pillow between the cast and her head. And again I drift, sniffing Laura's sweet peroxide hair. Sleep is ageless and painless, if death is like sleep it's not too bad, but I don't think it is. It's nothing.

Nurse Oprah is saying, "This is not a motel, honey wake up."

She shakes Laura and wakes her up. Laura wakes and gives me a little kiss, I can smell last night on her breath.

"I'll see you in court babe, it's gonna be okay."

Now there are little white fur hairs on my bed. I wonder why am I so lucky, to get away with everything. I need to get to the Buddhist place. I need to give up. I need something bigger than me to give up to. But I want to go with Laura, to follow decadence to its logical end. Like Hesse's Siddhartha, don't avoid, pass through. R.D Lang was onto it, don't repress, allow it to be, pass through it, like a cold, don't try to fight it, let it go to its logical end and come out cured in the end, or maybe not cured. Let the will to survive express itself. Unless it causes pain and hardship to others, which I've already done.

*The Three Pillars of Zen*, *The Tao Te Ching*, Ouspensky, Gurdjieff's *Tales*

STEPHEN JAY GOLDBERG

*of Beelzebub*, and hundreds of books that seemed like enlightenment at the moment but always getting smashed back to step one, even the twelve steps of AA. All those nights, years of nights looking for answers, so damn alone, book in hand, posing in front of bathroom mirrors, like a weight lifter or a great swimmer or a porno star. Studying Freud and Jung, lonely books upon books, words of brilliance on cold black and white pages. Always wanting the same desperate answer, that it's okay but it is not okay, it will never be okay. Because we all end up corpses, dead nothings, some remembered like Mozart or Rembrandt but even they lay rotting, stinking, like me or Laura or Neeta or kids, the hottest babes, the smartest men, some of them blowing their brains out, some literally, some a slow torture. Just nothing. Gone.

Freud thought it was all sex, it's all death, the big sexy avoidance, death. As if I have any answers, my mind is blown, my paintings are burnt, I'm old and ugly, ugly to myself. I hate people for their false comfort. Their boring non-passion, non-communication, uninteresting non-vitality. That's the shit that makes me lonely, makes me do what I do. And more and more I feel like I'm the only one left, not in terms of nature, but in terms of the human race, the human mind. All egocentric and self-centered. The "what can I get" idiot way of being. I can only be what I want the race to be by example.

So Laura says to me, "I have this sweet place outside of LA, Malibu. You want to go there with me? I'll take care of you Sid, like I didn't do for my father. So let me take care of you. We'll both get healed."

More Freud father stuff. She's using me to resolve past pain. Shit, is that all we do? More acting out for me, more false hope for her. Another beginning heading for another disappointment. I hate this analyzing crap. I would be better off in jail. To be in a real physical prison. That might be the Buddhist place I'm looking for, not the prison of my own mind and out of control emotions.

Now Laura is pretty hot, in fact very hot. I trust her in that she's like me, all fucked up but wanting to make things right and lucky. Lucky to have money and be beautiful but feeling her life is useless. This sort of crazed intelligence that turns on itself, like you want to put your hand into your head and rip it out because it's not on your side. It tricks you at every turn, every action to make things better gets you deeper in. I know she's doing this with her generous offer. And if I say yes, I'll go to Malibu, I'm only screwing myself more. Propagating the disease of need.

Now Oprah has left the hospital room. There's another guy in the room who's out of it, on some machine that's making this sloshing sound. He has some tube down his throat. I try not to look at him. Laura gets on top of me and the covers. She opens her fur coat and pulls down her black top. She has these beautiful enlarged nipples and these sweet breasts. The kind that you never see, where the nipple starts too early. She says "Please Sidney, we're gonna be okay. You're brave, I'm brave, we can fix it." Then she takes off her shades and looks into my eyes. It's like I can see into her brain, yet can't identify her eye color. Her eyes are all teary and red. I don't want to hear myself say, why me, so I hold it in. Just like I always have. She puts her breasts in my face and says, "We're gonna be okay."

In comes the nurse, a new one, a white on white one. I say my wife is just leaving. We have a sweet kiss that sort of smells from that sweet stuff like anisette that I never drink, but it smells sweet, she smells sweet.

I don't like planes but I'm on one. The court was a fast ten-minute deal, I didn't say a word. Laura had this real cool lawyer. I was more concerned about the pain in my arm under the cast. The judge thought the whole thing was a waste of time, he looked really bored, like let's get on to some real crime. Now like I said planes scare the hell out me, overactive mind stuff. Not only that but I know I should go home. So Laura gets us drinks and it's really dark out there in the sky. Laura lights a smoke and everyone goes nuts, she gives me a few sucks at it. The stewardess or flight attendant comes over and tells us you can't smoke on domestic flights, and Laura asks if this isn't a flight to Paris, this babe says no and you have to put out the cigarette.

I'm wearing the hospital clothes underneath my regular clothes, I figure I'll be right back there, so I'll save the LA people the trouble. Now Laura is like this goddess, she tells me how I'm going to love this place. On the little menu she draws a picture of the house and the sea. I have the window seat and I hate it. I see nothing, just black. No clouds, no nothing. I get this awful feeling like I have to get off this plane. My heart starts to pound. My arm under the cast is pounding, I can't swallow. I'm sweating. I try to say something that I can't get out. This being in the sky stuff is bad.

A double Wild Turkey appears on that stupid tray. I shoot it down. I feel better. She holds my hand, Laura does. "Sidney we're almost home. We're going to be okay."

I can't talk. I'm in trouble. I don't know what's going on.

# – eleven –

NINETY-NINE PERCENT OF THE THINGS I DEAL WITH I HAVE NO idea how they work, this plane, the radio, the TV remote, the cars, the credit cards, electricity, the phone, the goddamn sun in the sky, my own body, gravity, even the clothes I'm wearing, none of it, I don't goddamn get it. Nobody does, there are explanations, yeah but nobody really gets it, really understands. So what the hell good is the brain, is it just there to drive us nuts and that's what it's doing? We say, that's a tree, a bird, the sky. Oh yeah, we're great at naming things and we have some insane idea that by giving something a name we know what it is. Oh here's a plane that's cool, here's the subway, that's cool, there's Laura, this is me. Then some scientist says it's all atoms, oh yeah atoms, cool now I get it. Or it's all chemistry, microns, quarks, black holes, circuits, DNA. I don't get it, the more I think the more confusing it gets. So I figure there is no understanding, it's all phony, the concept of understanding is a lie. Then the big deal of death. Up in this plane, stuck in this piece of shit can, what else is there to think about, what else is there ever to think about except death. Thinking about a time when it's impossible to think or be. I don't get why the whole human race isn't obsessed with it. Maybe they are, maybe that's why we build these unforgiving machines.

The forgiving thing is, the thing that turns off the useless intellect is when I look over at Laura and see her open blouse and a little skin, or the hot flight attendant bend over and I see some thigh. The intellect has a little shut down, like the urinary canal when sperm want to come through. Little internal battles. Even that is totally incomprehensible to the human mind. Screw explanations, screw the human mind, there is no real understanding. I don't know why my mind is racing like this. See I lost the thought when I thought of my mind being my mind. The discomfort of the seat, of the situation. I don't know why this woman is taking me on this ride. I don't know why I'm here.

Something happens where the moment seems like forever, then we touch down, another horror to make it through.

The cab drives up a long driveway. It's dawn. There are all these flowers along the driveway. The cab goes off, Laura pays him. Then the sound of birds. It's warm, summer, the sun just coming up.

"The pool Sidney. We need to be cleansed before we sleep."

Her clothes come off so easily, like they were never meant to be there in the first place. I have trouble untying my shoes. She's bent down doing it for me, this beautiful shape, hair, back and hips. I lean back and look at the sky. So far, so far from anything. Seeing the clouds float as the sun comes up.

"Your cast Sidney."

"Screw it."

"You'll sink."

"So I sink, arm first."

The water is warm and safe, so unlike the plane. Real water, real air. I sink to the bottom and watch her float over me. Then float up for air and sink and float and sink and float, watching Laura fly. Feeling little stings where my cuts are. The air and the water are the same temperature.

We walk up a blue carpeted stairway and fall into a sweet silky bed. Laura gives me a bubbly drink and a shot of cognac and a few pills, then pulls herself next to me and I fall asleep to her talking, saying how we're going to be okay and telling a long complicated story. She asks me if I know where I am. I think I answer that I don't. I try to say, thank you.

## twelve

IT COULD HAVE BEEN DAYS OR WEEKS. THE ROOM IS ALL BLUE, it's night, there are candles burning all around me. I go to touch my head and my hair feels jelled, combed straight back.

"Drink this Sidney, it's a fresh fruit shake, so you don't shake, lots of B vitamins. You're in LA. You slept for a day and a half. I've invited a rabbi here to talk to you, after we have breakfast. Okay? Sidney, is that okay?"

"Yeah it's good."

"I figure he can answer some questions for you. I'd like to give you a B12 shot, it's good for you. Is that okay?"

"Yeah it's good."

"Do you remember my name?"

"Yeah, Laura. Laura why are you doing this?"

"It's for me, as well as it for you. Turn over so I can give you the shot."

And bam she does it, a little slap on the ass, the shot, then this sweet kiss right on the ass, then a smile.

"It's for the alcohol and whatever other crap you put into yourself. Let's take a few days, okay Sidney, we can always go back. Now you give me a shot, B12, you just pop it in and push the little plunger."

She lies down next to me and pulls up her little white robe and hands me the needle.

"Just punch it into my cheek and push the plunger, it's vitamins."

Now I have never pierced the flesh of anything, but I do it, push the little needle in her perfect ass and push in the plunger.

"Good job Sidney. I want you to meet Rabbi Grossman. Rabbi! Come in here."

Laura pulls down her little silk gown.

"Sidney, this is Rabbi Grossman." Then she leaves the bedroom giving me a little flash of her sweet ass and thighs.

In walks the rabbi. He's the whole deal. Dressed in black, black-gray beard. Fedora black hat with curls hanging out the side.

"I was Sammy Davis' rabbi. Does that mean anything to you?"

"Yes. Sammy Davis was the best."

"He had questions about God. Do you have questions about God?"

"I do, yes a lot of questions."

"Sammy lost an eye, he needed to know why."

"Yeah, Sammy was the best"

"Let's cut the crap Sidney, are you a Jew?"

"I think so."

"Do you know what that means."

"No."

"Then you're not."

"But if you ask a dog what a dog is, he can't tell you. Does that make him not a dog?"

"We're not talking about dogs. We're talking about you. Dogs can't speak or think."

"Good for them. I can speak but not think."

"Jews are thinkers and thinking you can't think makes you a thinker. Sidney I'm not here to debate with you, I'm here to help you. Laura says you're a very troubled man."

"And is Laura paying you to talk to me?"

"Yes because she cares about you. Do you believe in God?"

"Give me a break, Rabbi."

"God believes in you."

"I'm sure he doesn't. He might have believed in Sammy Davis Junior but not me."

"Why not you?"

"Because God likes celebrities, in his own image. He is the ultimate celebrity."

"Sidney I can see you're in trouble."

"Listen pal, my grandfather and grandmother died in the camps, where was God then, my mother never forgave him, she had bad nights and bad dreams and had big questions. Are you going to explain that to me? Where the hell was God? In a fucking sauna!"

"It was a test, Sidney."

"Bullshit. Listen Rabbi, I want to hold on to something but not some outdated ritual crap about not eating dairy with meat, or covering your head with a little cap, you have some truth to give me, lay it on to me."

"The truth is there is an ultimate power, look at your hands, the incredible detail of the skin, the fingerprints, the brilliant design. The ability to hear me speaking or the complicated system that lets you answer me and understand the connection of my words. Did you create that Sidney, the detail of being able to see me and my hat and beard? Did you create that ability? The complicated electrical system, that no human can create, the flowers and the animals, the sky, the universe? Do you want to take credit for that? Hey Sidney, did you make that?"

"No one made it, it just happened."

"Just happened."

"Yeah, just happened."

"The ultimate accident."

"Yeah."

"So the impossible can just happen."

"Yeah."

"Just to screw with you."

"What?"

"The impossible happened just to screw with your mind, to confuse you. Sidney, give up. You can't even take credit for the mind you think you can't think with. The thoughts you have are a gift of a force that is not you, you have to get that. The mechanics that let you think your anti-thoughts were built by God, not you. You need some peace, don't you?"

"I'm so tired but I think you're a phony."

"You don't trust anyone, do you?"

"No, or anything."

"Do you want to?"

"Are you a rabbi or a shrink?"

"A rabbi, a man of God, just like you. The only thing is I know it and you don't."

"How are you going to help me."

"How would you like me to help you?"

"I'd like you to give me some money, lots of money. What do you say?"

"Well Sidney, maybe I'd like to buy one of your paintings. You're an artist, aren't you."

"Who told you that?"

"Laura did."

"I don't remember telling her. Besides, you can't. I burned all my paintings."

"Why did you do that."

"Because they were crap, bullshit. No one liked them."

"I might have."

"I doubt it."

"Art comes through God, it's a gift, just because no one likes it doesn't lessen its value. No one liked Van Gogh or Schoenberg or Stravinsky or John Cage or many others, not at first. Now I'll never get to see your paintings, that makes me sad. Sammy told me they didn't like him at first, a little funny looking black man. See, but he knew he was touched by God."

"How'd he know that?"

"He told me he could feel it. And he told me how much he loved the feeling of performing."

"I'm not that talented."

"Sidney, why don't you give yourself a chance?"

"I hate that Laura is paying you to do this."

"Fine, I won't take any money. When you're a successful artist make a donation, to those more unfortunate than you. Okay?"

"Yeah, okay. But I don't think I can paint, ever again. My wife, Anita, never could take the time to look at my work, not really look. It was like she said once, she didn't get it. Now every night I slept with this woman, and we make love, have sex and all, but I feel castrated because she doesn't get it."

"And at the moment of creation?"

"Fuck! At the moment of creation it's the best. Exciting, alive. Then I look at the stuff on the next day when I wake up and it's crap, a waste of paint, a nothing, a waste of time, these lines, white lines on black, that make me nothing. Then I drink the last of the whiskey and am pissed off at everybody and everything."

"Because you imagine it was not in the image of the creator."

"Because it doesn't look good. Fuck the creator. It looks bad, untrue."

"You put your life into your art, didn't you?"

"Into my bullshit, yeah. A complete waste of time."

"You might be right, but you have now to change it all, do you want that?"

"Yeah."

"So let's do it, you and me, we'll change it all right now. Can you do that?"

"I don't know, I don't know what you want me to do."

"You just need to do what I ask you to do. What God asks you to do."

"So you're speaking for God."

"Believe it or not, yes I am. You trust me, you trust God. Sidney I'm not trying to sell you anything. I'm here for you. You've made yourself too important to yourself so you've come to a dead end. Does that sound right?"

"Yeah, so what."

"So you're turning on yourself, like an animal that self-devours and you can do that if you want to. I'm just here to give you another choice."

"And what's that?"

"To forget yourself and make everything outside yourself more important than yourself, and I mean everything."

"That's how I already feel."

"No, you feel everyone and everything is better than you, better, not more important but better, that's why you feel so bad about yourself."

"Do you think I'm more important than you?"

"Yes, absolutely. Yes, to me you are."

"And what does that give you."

"It gives me freedom. Sidney I was a hedonist, a sensualist, even a drug addict, a materialist, I had my own airplane and a subscription to *Gourmet Magazine*, I had four wives at the same time and lots of girlfriends, the whole deal and I was where you are now."

"And where is that?"

"On empty. On desperation. On confusion. It's up to you. If you want to move on you can, I'm here to help. If you want to stay where you are it's okay. Whatever you want."

"You know what I think."

"I don't Sidney but I'd like to hear it."

"I think you should fuck off. I think you're full of shit, that's what I think. Rabbi."

"That's too bad, I'm here for you, if you need me."

"Yeah. I don't want to talk to you."

"You're ready Sidney. What happened to your arm?"

"I broke it in an automobile accident."

"You're lucky to be alive, aren't you?"

"I don't know about that."

"Why do you think God in his infinite wisdom saved you."

"To listen to your bullshit?"

"Why do you think you're not paralyzed?"

"So I can take a swing at you."

"Is that what you want to do?"

"I might."

"Go on."

"Just fuck off."

"Do you know why you're so angry."

"Yeah, I do."

"Please Sidney, tell me."

"Because it's all so fucking hopeless."

"Is that why you burned all your paintings?"

"I don't know, okay, okay and neither do you. So spare the explanations."

"I think you've been spared enough. Why didn't you go with the Buddhists?"

"How do you know about that?"

"I know all about it."

"Really."

"Yes really. You're on a search, the ultimate search."

Now I look into his eyes for the first time and there are tears slowly running out, dripping into his gray mustache and beard. I take a cigarette out of my pocket, and he lights it for me. I offer him one, he takes it and lights it. We sit there smoking and looking at each other. He gets up and gets us an ashtray and puts it between us. And it does seem like some kind of ancient ritual, like a peace pipe. It's like I'm glued to his eyes, I feel my throat getting tight like I want to cry. I haven't cried or thrown up, maybe not since I was a kid.

He starts to speak very slowly, taking deep, delicate puffs of the Lucky Strike.

"Sidney, I'm seventy-six years old, and yes, it is, as you say, hopeless, this need to transcend ourselves, that is what it is, to pass ourselves by and become part of the truth or the goodness or the ugliness of the truth. Do you hear me, Sidney?"

"Unfortunately yes."

"I have a gift for you. A way to clear up all the confusion and depression. Would you like that?"

"Rabbi, I'd like a drink, I'd like to get it on with Laura. Then get some sleep. You're a good man, a beautiful man. But I can't stop till I'm at the end."

"Sidney, a Jew's realization comes through the mind, the brain, then the heart and that realization borders on insanity, it's a thin line, a very dangerous trip, if it's real. I'm going to leave now. No charge, except you owe me a painting, a new painting, okay?"

"Yeah, okay

# - thirteen -

SO IN COMES LAURA IN THIS LITTLE HOT RED ROBE. SHE ASKS me if I like the rabbi. I tell her yes, he's okay. She repeats the whole deal about him being Sammy Davis' rabbi and how he did Sammy's funeral and names all the movie stars that were there. Then she tells me this great story about how she made it with Sinatra after some big benefit for crippled children, how he did her in the bathroom, her bent over a toilet seat and Frank getting it on or off, how cool.

The thing I don't like are the implants. I think, who am I? But the implants are bad. But she is such a good lover, I mean slow, really slow. I like the chemical smell of her blond hair. I wonder if she can feel her nipples through the implants. I find the little scars around her breasts and find the rabbi's eyes and the tears. Which is good because it all gets so slow. I see the same tears dropping down on my chest as the man of God. Laura so hot above me.

Hot breasts bouncing. Wanting everything. I'm afraid she's going to break me, smash me, smash me in half. Then as I look at her beautiful jumping face all red and hot. Jumping on me like a crying woman. Tough guy that I am, Laura does it, does me in, and beautiful sleep. How sweet to hold her next to me. To listen to her breath. The light coming up. The little breathing sounds. The strange sounds of the LA birds. I'm lost, gone. I have the last little hit of blow on the night table and fall into dreams so deep and sweet.

I wake up to the sound of a hair dryer blowing on my cast. It's not Laura with the hair dryer, but a little Japanese woman. She shuts off the dryer and gives me a fruit shake to drink and two vitamin pills.

"Powder last night not blow, synthetic heroin. You sleep good?"

"Yes, very good."

"Rabbi leave book for you. *Tao Te Ching*. Good book. You know?"

"I've forgotten it."

"It says, 'Give up learning and put an end to your troubles.' Pretty funny stuff."

"Yeah, funny stuff."

"Where's Laura?"

"In garden, putting end to her troubles."

She wraps plastic around my cast.

"Don't want to get cast wet in hot tub. Hot tub just outside."

"What, did I die and go to heaven?"

"Could be. My is name Jaki. Put on robe and go soak in hot tub."

She gives me this white silk robe, Jesus now I know I'm dead.

"Then we make love, if you want."

We go downstairs out the back door onto a redwood deck with a hot tub built into it. She takes my robe and helps me in.

"Sidney, wash away troubles in the unnamable."

There's all these flowers and humming birds and palm trees. I lay there in the warm bubbling water, looking at the sky. For the first time for as long as I can remember, thoughts don't come, they start to, and then get dispersed and float off into the sky. Jaki has gone off and there's a little black bearded dog sitting there looking at me. He has one of those wise half-smiling dog faces. Just sitting there a few feet from the hot tub, his eyes these sweet black pools. His eyes, the sky, that's all there is. Thoughts begin, like, "This is so..." Then dispersed. Like; "Why is this..." Dispersed. I try to describe to myself what is going on. I can't do it, it all floats away, yet everything is so incredibly clear. I'm not watching and analyzing what's going on. I'm in it, part of it. Same as the dog and the trees and the sky and the flowers and birds, time and the warm water I'm soaking in. There is no difference between us, there is no "us." We're all into it. So is everything that ever happened and that will ever happen. I'm not thinking this stuff. It just is. The smiling dog gets up, walks down the three steps off the deck to a palm tree and takes a piss and keeps looking at me while he does and it's like this wondrous most beautiful, perfect thing that has ever occurred in all the history of the everything. On his little legs he comes back on the deck and sits down and looks me. All of us knowing he's done a really good thing. Inspired, I do the same in the warm water. A good thing. Time has at last stopped.

It stays stopped for as long as time can stay stopped, like forever. As soon as I try to hold onto it it's gone. Smiling-dog walks off the deck and Jaki appears.

"Time to get out. Don't want to make Sidney soup."

I try to speak, say something clever but I can't.

"You want smoke, cigarette?"

I shake my head, no.

"Laura says I give you rub. Okay?"

Again I can't speak, I shake my head yes. Jaki dries me off with a soft white towel. I try to wonder if I've had a stroke but happily can't complete the thought. She finishes drying me, puts the smooth robe on me and takes me into a small darkened room and helps me onto a massage table.

"I make you feel good, okay?"

I can't answer and lay face down on the table. She starts at my shoulders with this sweet warm oil, her hands have all this power but the softness of butterflies. She makes this very soft humming sound as she rubs me, going deeper and deeper into my body. Again time stops. She does my arms, my feet, calves, thighs, ass.

"Is good?"

I can't answer.

Then I feel something going into me. At first so small and subtle, like her tiny pinky. Then I feel her slowly getting bigger inside me, her hand reaching up into my heart. So strong, pulling my heart out. Pulling out all the pain it's caused. I feel her long black Asian hair drifting at the base of my spine, this black different world breeze on what use to be my body, no time, only unknown sensations, this deepness into me. All oil and smoothness.

She turns me over on my back, like I don't even know she's doing it. It's all so gentle and filled with power. She kisses me, first on the mouth and it's an unknown taste, something so far away from anything I have ever known, like some earth-dirt that things grow in. Then she stands over me, her ankles on my ears so I can look up inside her. I see this sunlight coming out of her. This beautiful sunlight beaming down on me. A ray of goodness pouring down on me. I drink it in, not unlike the sweet fruit shake that she had made for me. She lowers herself so delicately onto my lips. An unknown different bearded mouth so sweet and good, drinking in the sun. She, the beautiful Asian Jaki, puts her hand between my legs and slides me into her, nipples more extended than I have ever seen, so hard and pointed on my chest, she kisses me so soft, her tongue so deep inside my mouth then throat. I look up at her eyes so beautiful so knowing so unlike anything I've ever looked into. Little droplets of white sweat dropping off her the tips of her nipples. She says, looking into eyes that are so new and unknown, "Now!" and it's so easy to let go. So perfect to love some other world. I'm gone. Then she slides down on me and starts it all over, she's slow and hot. It keeps going on over and over. Time goes, it all goes. Orgasm after orgasm till it loses all meaning. And each time she looks at me like we can go further. Push as far as you can push it. Get as hot as we can get, and there's more and more. She does every conceivable sexual act and has orgasm after orgasm, orgasms that I can feel and see. I am put away, I never had anything close to the repeated orgasms, over and over again, she getting hotter and hotter. Me getting harder and bigger after each one. Everything unknown. She says something softly in a far-away Asian language. Something I might have gone all my life without hearing. She slowly slides what seems like my whole body, my whole existence out of her. She's given me back to myself. I know I can't hold onto her, I can't even try. And she's gone.

I know I should be wondering why this is happening, or if it's happening. But laying on this table, this bed, feeling gravity pulling me safely towards it. I imagine the oceans flying off the planet into space. One mass lack of explanation for anything.

Laura comes into the darkened room. I used to sing the song, "Laura." "Laura is the face on the barroom floor." I just see her silhouette with the light behind her. With her is the half-smiling dog, both backlit.

"Sidney, you look very beautiful, like a man who's just had surgery."

She helps me off the table and takes me through the open door. It's night. We go into a room off the deck. We stand in front of a huge mirror. The room is all lit by hundreds of candles. She lets her red robe fall to the floor. We're both naked. The dog in his black and gray fur.

"Look Sidney, that's us. That's you."

And I look. I start at my feet.

"Take your time Sidney."

I see the years, the pain, the power I fought for. It's like the dog and Laura are with me, looking at this thing. This me thing. I don't judge, I can't judge. The arms, the legs, chest, hairs, prick, face, so complicated, the face. All the openings. Nose, mouth, ears, eyes, inside the forehead and the graying hair, the brain. The terrible brain, that does all the harm. I can see my back in the mirror across the room, and Laura and the dog.

"Move Sidney, it's okay to see yourself moving."

I remember the book I did studies from when I was in art school, "The human figure in motion." I remember how the studies of the women would make me hot. And how art made me hot.

Then we start to move, around the room, all mirrors. I am a man, a man's body, Laura's a woman, the dog a dog. Laura takes me by the hand and we stand close to a mirror. She holds her breasts from underneath. Sticks them out more than they were already sticking. Like two gunner turrets on a battleship.

"You know why I did this Sidney? Why I got these implants? To improve on nature. I keep them as a reminder about bad ideas. The physicalization of a double bad idea. I keep them as a reminder. And you know what? They turn men on, so it keeps me clued in to the values of our society. That's pretty sad don't you think?"

I can't speak. Not yet.

"So I hate these tits, but I did it, like I did a lot of things to make things better. What about you Sidney. Look at yourself, you want surgery, lipo on your belly, a bigger cock, a hair implant, I can afford it. Make you look twenty years younger. You look okay to me, natural, sexy, beautiful. But we can do a makeover, if you want."

Then she goes down on me, sucks me in front of the mirrors, and I don't hold back. I see her beautiful back and ass in multi reflections. I look at myself, the body of me, the face of me. Every time my eyes close I open them and watch in the mirror, like a sand crab, who reproduce in a similar way. I let myself easily come in her mouth, watching her ass and open legs in the mirror. The hairs around her opening. In the mirror I see a young man, strong and dangerous. Her body is all backbone and thick sweet ass. I count the vertebrae. Sweet Laura. How beautiful opening her cheeks and hearing the Guru pant and weep. Her opening is not fixed or implanted and the juices that pour out are all honest. I collapse on a red mat on the floor, I watch the fall in the mirror, as if in slow motion. It seems ecstasy and passing out is becoming a way of life. Again time fades.

# - fourteen -

AT FIRST, I DON'T RECOGNIZE HIM, THE RABBI, HE'S WEARING
some sort of outdated cabana suit. Brightly colored flowered shirt with
shorts to match and a straw fedora hat, but he still has on his black shoes
and socks. He pulls a transparent plastic chair up to the head of my mat.
He hands me one of those fruits shakes in the same thick frosted glass.

"Laura and I had a talk. We agree. It's time to call your wife, make
amends. What do you think Sidney? She might be worried."

"What is this, AA?"

"Have you been to AA, Sidney?"

"Once for half a meeting."

"This isn't AA."

I feel the old Sidney, the Sidney of Resistance coming back.

"You don't need to hurt people anymore. Have we hurt you? Laura,
Jaki, Buddy and I."

"Who's Buddy?"

"Buddy, the dog."

I look over at Buddy the half-smiling dog. He's sitting there all prim
and proper, looking very serious.

"What do you say, how about we give Anita a call?"

I realize I'm lying there naked, looking up at him.

"I don't really want to talk to her."

"You want a drink Sidney, to get up the nerve."

"I wouldn't mind a drink."

He goes over to a transparent table, it looks like glass, I hadn't noticed
it, on it is a huge bottle of Absolute Vodka, there's a glass ice bucket, he
pours me a glass of it on the ice, all transparent except for the blue word,
Absolute. He takes off his straw fedora, exposing his little black scull

cap on his almost hairless head. Everything he does has this ritual about it, like it's so very important, every detail of expended energy has some meaning, some subtext. Buddy the dog follows his every movement with his dog eyes.

"Here you go Sidney, drink up."

He takes the finished shake glass from me and hands me the Absolute.

"Here Sidney, you might need this."

He covers me in a blue soft sheet. The vodka tastes smooth and cold and hot at the same time. Only my feet are exposed.

"Good, isn't it?"

"Yes."

He walks to the foot of the mat.

Then this pain, the Man of God kicks the arch of my right foot so all I feel is pain, this red all-powerful pain, then again, both feet, his black pointed shoes into my arches, up my spine into my head. I drop my drink.

"Sidney let me get you a refill. You've had a little accident."

Buddy the dog paces, watches, and sends out little whining sounds. Now he brings me a fresh glass, but the top of the glass is all razor-sharp broken edges. I take a sip and can feel the warm blood running from my lips and see the contents of the glass, the Absolute turning a beautiful red, the mixture of the blood and the alcohol has this perfect taste, the perfect mixed drink. Buddy is now into a full bark. Then the Rabbi puts his black shoe on my cast, on my arm, and it falls apart, exposing innocent skin. Then his black shoe is on my newborn arm, the arm that the Beemer smashed. I get up and point the edge of the broken glass at his bearded aged face. I see the fear in his eyes. And I smash the broken sharp edge of the glass into his face, his beard, his mouth, his eyes. I pound it in, till his face is all blood and bone, I smash the horrible bones of his face, put my knee into his balls, over and over again as I pound away at his skull, till it's all pulp. I rip the little skullcap off his head and put it down his throat, my arm down his throat, I can feel the bones ripping apart, the throat, the horror of his ugly old body. I smash his ribs and hear the breath and the useless words coming out of him. His blood is all over me. Man of God in a cabana suit. I take off his black shoes and put them on my feet and smash his dead weak old body as if it were mine. I rip off the stupid cabana outfit, and grab his old gray balls and what's left of his prick. All hopeless and limp.

The dog is all barking, I tell it to shut up. He licks the blood off me and starts to eat the body, I sit on the mat and watch. I get up and give one more group of heavy kicks to the Rabbi's pulpy head. Buddy the dog looks up at me, I give him a little kiss on his nose, when he puts his tongue out, I grab it, and kiss it and point to the Rabbi, he looks a little afraid. He eats his dinner. Old and ugly as it is. The dog looks at me, belly full, he knows he's next, I can't, I don't, I open the door and he runs off. Again the pass out, next to the pulpy man of God, I hold his body, his bones, the blue sheet with red stains. The LA birds sing. No I don't want to make a phone call. You fuckers want to break me. Please break me. I kiss the skull of the broken body I've killed. The pure white bone above the hairline. You my friend, can't tell me what to do, or kick me with your black unforgiving shoes. I close my eyes, I feel my body shaking, heart pounding, then nothing.

When I come to, the room is clean, the body is gone. I'm relieved maybe it didn't happen, but I feel the throbbing pain on my cast-less arm and the burning on the bottoms of my feet. On the wall hangs the blue sheet, with beautiful red abstract designs, incredible forms. The painting I owe the rabbi.

I'm covered with a smooth black satin sheet that replaces the blue one. I study the blue and red painting for a long time. Everything is quiet, so very silent. No doubt the police are next, then prison.

Laura and Jaki enter the room wearing matching black silk kimonos. Buddy follows.

Laura speaks; "He was old Sidney, he didn't have long to live, maybe a month or two. Cancer eating his liver."

"I'm sorry."

"He went too far, didn't he?"

"I don't know."

"Your arm looks pretty bad. Jaki will fix it."

Jaki puts some acupuncture needles in my shoulder. Puts some strong-smelling cream on my re-broken arm. The pain is gone, she mixes up some black plaster and applies a new black cast Then more needles around my ankles and rubs cream onto the bottoms of my feet and packs them in ice.

"When will the police be here to get me."

Jaki and Laura smile at each other. Buddy looks at one then the other, with his half-smile.

Laura says; "No police. He's already buried, we'll have a service tomorrow, if you're up to it."

"What are you, part of the old Manson gang?"

"I knew Charlie before he went nuts. Pretty intense guy. But a bit misguided. Sidney, it's easy to get off the track. Like Dylan said, a little 'twist of fate.' We're here to save you. Whatever it takes."

"And why me?"

"Because you're ready. And fate brought us together."

I feel the black plaster, tightening on my arm.

"That is a beautiful painting, Rabbi Grossman would be proud to own it.

"Ironic, isn't it?"

"It's okay."

Now Jaki has put my feet in ice, and put large white plastic socks over them, something I'd wear to Antarctica. Where I don't want to go. My feet feel numb, gone.

"Sidney, we have a wheelchair for you, don't let it frighten you. Your feet are pretty broken up, we'll help you up."

Now they drop their kimonos, both naked, the dog Buddy leaves, tail drooping, and they lift me into the wheelchair that Jaki has brought in. Jaki is not that small in height as I had imagined. They are both the same. They lift me into this ancient wheelchair, all wicker and bamboo. Their breasts touch together as they lift me, careful to not upset the black satin sheet. In the chair they kiss each other right next to my face. Jaki adjusts the leg rests so my legs are spread. The black plaster holding my broken right arm.

They kiss each other right over me, tongues in mouth. They wheel me out on the redwood deck. I know me being helpless makes them hotter and hotter. Then they both get on me, rubbing their nipples along my thighs. All mouth and love. I come all over them, their beautiful faces. They drink it in and then make each other come, all excited, all mouth and love. They wheel me in towards a sweet large bed and fall asleep next to me.

# - fifteen -

THE GRAVE IS NEXT TO A FLOWER GARDEN, THEY WHEEL ME
out to it. There are all these strangers around. Fifty or sixty people dressed
in funeral garb. It's bright sunlight. Laura has dressed me in an awful
black suit, white shirt, black tie, with the rabbi's black shoes on my feet.
The same shoes that I kicked his head in with. I ask her for sunglasses,
she says she doesn't have any. Everyone else is wearing sunglasses. Except
for the speaker, a young pale guy who is wearing a black baseball hat, on
backwards with his black suit. He has these thin gray eyes and wrinkled
forehead. He talks in this nasal voice.

"My father was a great man, a man who gave up himself for the good
of others. He discovered goodness late in life, it was his life's work, to
show us the way, the way the song is supposed to go, honest and true.
Sammy Davis made his most beautiful albums in tribute to dad. My
father believed people were good. That life has this swing to it, a beat
of goodness. He loved the big bands, the community of notes, being
in a trumpet section, a saxophone section, a trombone section. Or the
drummer who sets it up. The rhythm of life. He's there in the ground in
front of us. A dead man, gone. Thanks dad for all the love and caring.
And most of all goodbye. We will miss you. I want to read you a note
from Frank Sinatra, the chairman of the board. It says, 'Rabbi Grossman,
you cook. Sorry I couldn't be there for your coda, swing out, you are a
good guy, so Sammy told me. Frank Sinatra.'"

Now everybody is in tears. I really don't care. I'm hot in this
wheelchair and black suit. I think I see some movie stars. Like Cher and
Jack Nicholson and Elizabeth Taylor. But I'm not sure if it's them. All I
know is I'm hot and can't walk and have no sunglasses. Laura is next to

me, hand holding my shoulder. She whispers in my ear. "It's good that you killed him. It's good he's gone. He was a prick."

Then they all leave, except the son who had done the eulogy. The wheelchair is tough to move on the grass, Laura trying to push it. Son-of-Rabbi says to me, "Sorry for your troubles." The crowd dispersed.

I'm sitting there alone in the ancient wheelchair. Laura and the rest of them off and gone. I'm in a little ditch, stuck, the wheels stuck. Looking towards the rabbi's grave, no one to wheel me. My thought is screw them, looking at the grave of the man I've killed. The birds don't give a damn, they sing, hang out as if nothing has happened. Death of a human, who gives a damn. A man of God, who gives a damn.

I can't move the chair. I drop myself off it and hit the newly dug grave. Sorry Rabbi.


Then an arm on me, then another. Cops all over the place, they look like kids, corny sunglasses, tight fitting shirts, little pistols on their belts. One of the kids reads me my rights. Blah, blah, blah, for the murder of...And they carry me into the cop car, handcuffs and all, they keep saying, "For the murder of.".Blah, blah, blah. As if I give a damn. They all look so neat and clean and costumed. Well-trimmed. So serious, like they don't want to make any mistakes. "You have a right to a lawyer." In the car I look through the window, back at the wheelchair, empty, alone, stuck, just sitting there. No Laura, no smiling dog, no hot oriental massage girl. And off we go. Me in the back of the black and white, handcuffed and all. Two black and whites behind me. This procession. All I can say is, I have nothing to say. The cemetery behind me, the Rabbi and all the dead, safe and sound. Me not so safe and sound in yet another tin can, off to the can.

The ride takes forever, I look at the LA scenery. The young cop says, "Murder one is bad." I ask him, "Where did you get off track with that awful haircut." I mean it's ugly in the back, too trimmed. So now it's jail.

They get me out of the car, careful not to bang my head. It can be dangerous getting in and out of cars with handcuffs on. Before I know it I'm in this little cell, no bars, all cement and glass with a little shiny silver toilet and sink. How nice they thought of everything, just like the Holiday Inn, except without the horrible paintings. I wonder if the same architect designed both of them. There's a few pieces of writing on the wall, one says, "Life dies" and others not so interesting. One says, "Help," the other, "Fuck Everything." Which I agree with. I feel hungry, like I want a big liverwurst sub with mustard and pickles and tomatoes. I slam on the glass window of the steel door but no one responds. I can see them in this booth, sort of like a Star Trek home base, except no women. I remember the lion in the Bronx Zoo, a spectacle of creatures more beautiful and more innocent than I, all falling apart. A little kid throwing a Mars Bar at him, the lion, the Mars bar in it's wrapper, the lion looking at the bar code, not wanting to touch it.

I lay down on the slab of the bed. There's stuff written on the ceiling. More like scratched in. Like, "I'm not a bad person but she is a bitch." And "I've never hurt anyone." There's even one that says, "Bird Lives." My mother once told me when they circumcise Jews they send the foreskins to Ireland to grow cops. And the cops have me now, the foreskins. In this shit hole cell.

The Rabbi needed to die, he had this fucked up image of how life should be. If God was so cool and loving he wouldn't torture us like this. If there is a God he's a major prick who just gets off on his own power. To lead us into his death scene. To play games, an evil bastard who hates human beings and enjoys watching us on the kill, killing for some stupid belief about loving him so much. And we fall for that shit and die for that shit. These pricks have me now. I can't get free.

I look through the tiny window, out of the cage. Them in blue standing around, fat stomachs, making their shitty money. To have some crappy gas barbecue on their crappy Sunday day off. Ugly bastards. I'm glad I'm not them. If I could I would slap them around and make them face the truth, I would but they own me. The prisoner. Fuck, it's bad. I hate this. But it seems right. No they can't kill me, I'll kill myself. I'll slam my head on their ugly wall till it's dead, my mind. I'm sick of it. I lay on the slab and read the writing of those poor bastards that have been in this lockup before me. God, I want a party for all of us, on a sailboat, sailing off this fucking lockup. I don't care what the crime was. The crime is always need. Always needing more, to fill the empty hole in our guts. It fills my body, my mind, this unforgiving need for passion, for fire. Like it fills all of them, all of us. Settling for less, Fuck that. Let it kill me, let them kill all of us for being incomplete. And God can look down and say, "I told you so." We are the ugly, the ageless, the eternal. This rage is all there is, this power of life. Screw these walls. You can't ever hold me. Never ever. My fingernails scratch these walls writing hieroglyphics of past lives. You fuckers, you can't touch me. Come in here, torture me, you weak little punks. I have no reflection. I fall, as if a camera could record it. There is only white behind my eyes, the whiteness of nothing.

# — sixteen —

THE DOOR OPENS, A MAN IN A DARK SUIT, WHITE SHIRT, RED TIE with blue dots, tired eyes and gray thinning hair enters. I want to strangle him just for being human. For living this idiotic life. "I'm your lawyer, Sidney. Robert Eldridge," this tired voice says. He sits next to me on this shit mattress. I tell him I want a woman to sleep in this cell with me. He opens a leather briefcase filled with papers. "Sidney, you're in big trouble, I'm here to help. It seems you killed a man." I never want to look into a human face again. Into hopeless human eyes. And that sound of speech is sickening. My circumference of movement keeps closing in on me. I'm game for it, I surrender dear, like the old song says.

"I'm the best defense lawyer in LA. Your friend Laura hired me."

"I tell you Mister El."

"Bob, you can call me Bob."

"I tell you Bob, I'm already dead, do you understand that. I don't give a damn what they do to me. So tell Laura not to waste her money."

"It's a done deal, she wants me to send you back to your wife."

"Yeah well, that's very enlightened, Bob."

"Listen asshole, I don't lose cases. Tomorrow is the arraignment. I'm getting you out on bail. Five hundred thousand dollars."

Then "Bob" opens up his briefcase, reaches in and takes out two small blue pills, they have this interesting hexagram shape.

"Sidney, these pills will kill you in minutes, it's your choice. You want to play games, I have no time for that crap. You don't want to see the palm trees again or the great oceans of the world or a woman's breasts, it's fine with me. Here you go, you want to end it. Fine. I'm a busy man and a tired man. I'd like to go home, eat dinner and watch the Lakers game."

He puts the pills in my hand. I want to ask him if it's legal, to poison an inmate. Then I rethink the question. He's the lawyer.

"Well Sidney, I don't have a lot of time to play games with you. Take them and you'll be dead in twenty minutes, just as I leave the parking lot for dinner. I don't really see what Laura and her money see in you. You look like another loser to me."

I swallow the pills without water, without thinking.

"Why don't you take off pal. This life is one pain in the ass. You're a pain in the ass."

He just stands there, shakes his head and looks at me.

"I guess I believe you, Sidney. Looks like you're pretty fed up."

"Yeah, so goodbye."

"You just saved the state a lot of money and saved me a lot of time. Hope you enjoy the void."

"Yeah, the void looks pretty good."

He smiles and hands me a dollar bill and says, "Send me a postcard if they have any."

Jesus, I did it. It's over. I'm not even scared. I'll be out of here real soon. I won't cause anyone any more trouble. I can feel my heart beating real fast. I am a loser, a failure, a nothing. It's like that Zen thing, "Get realized or die." Maybe I'm doing both. This prick keeps looking at me. No one liked Hitler's paintings either. I didn't get that bad, as bad as Hitler did and I'm pretty bad. No one liked Vincent's work either except his brother. Maybe Theo didn't like it either but, he said he did, he cared and kept the stuff around. My work is smoke, up in the sky, it wasn't that good, I don't think it was. Mr. Eldridge is still staring at me.

"You better get out of here and ask them to cremate me."

"Sure, Sidney."

Now let's say I would have sold some stuff or Hitler became a popular German painter because of a Jewish agent who believed in him. Or Vincent sold his work and had a woman who loved him. It might be a different world. Or I believed in myself. Perceptions change.

He's still looking at me. I guess he knows what he's doing, he's an attorney, a big shot. He wants to watch me die, like a fly on flypaper or a roach in this roach motel. Imagine watching a client die, strapped down, getting his lethal injection or fried in the electric chair. Then going home and eating your lamb chops and watching some basketball game on your big screen TV and trying to care who wins. Knowing in your guts how cruel we are to each other. Some sad shit, we humans.

I've always taken the easy way out, like I'm doing now. Why didn't I paint on canvas, like Neeta said, or silk? I wanted them to come to me, embrace me and tell me how great I was. But I wasn't great. Maybe now, the last minute, the long ball, last play. Robert Eldridge, the lawyer, stands there and I want to draw him, paint him, his hopeless eyes, watching me about to die. That would be a great painting, in the style of Francis Bacon. The look on his face, these walls, all frozen, like time has stopped, a giant freeze frame.

I feel my heart pounding blood through me. This thing, this organ that I didn't put in, didn't insert. This thing is going nuts to survive. Something has happened, the separation of heart and mind. Like church and state. I feel all this strength, like I can power through these walls and dive into the Pacific and swim forever, down deep with the deep-sea creatures that we haven't yet seen. They have a good hiding place down there. Beyond any law, past any crime, great creatures, who's tiny brains are geared to the power of survival. To eat and fuck and swim. To move for the need to move. To eat other living creatures knowing there is no death only the continuum. You swallow me, I swallow you, we eat each other, devour each other to live and it doesn't matter who does who, it goes on till it ends, then it starts over, a billion light years, a few seconds. It's an impossible thing that's happened, thinking life, a life that thinks. Odds way against it, random accident after random accident. It all goes, with all this self-importance. I clench my fist and smash the wall. A few tiny pieces of plaster or whatever this shit house is fall. They make an unpredictable configuration on this stained floor. The stains of criminals.

This fucker is still in my cell, watching.

"GO!"

"It's sugar, the pills, nothing, Sidney. I wanted to see how troubled you are."

"You fucker."

"You're very troubled, it will help in court. A poor, sick depressed artist, you fit a very dumb prototype that has been sickening to me, because of your self-indulgence. Side A: the system. Side B: the anti-system. Side A, knowing how to work the system, ends up with swimming pools, hot houses filled with exotic flowers, nice automobiles, driven drunk or sober. Hot women or men, paid for or not paid for, the paid for ones do whatever you ask for, any act at any time, and my friend, the paid for lies are just as satisfying as the real stuff, maybe better, because the transaction is understood. No inhibited lie or fake emotion. It's a paid for deal, a business transaction. Sidney, you missed out. Because you had some faith that humanity was good. You're going to walk out of here into a nut house for a few months because I can convince the court that you're crazy and suicidal and because Laura is very rich and you were willing to die for your ideals. Your idealism is a bore. So you take care. I hope the sugar pills don't upset your stomach."

"You are one sadistic motherfucker."

"No Sidney, I'm one smart man who knows how to work the system.

I get paid a lot of money to do it."

"And what does all that money buy you, prick."

"Anything I want."

"Anything."

"Yes, anything, the best of anything. I like the best. I'll see you tomorrow. You'll be here, you're on suicide watch, you don't even have the choice of life and death."

"I can will myself to die."

"I don't think you have that much control over your mind."

Then he leaves, the cell door closes behind him. Poor tired man. Four walls, ceiling, floor. Six sided lock up. Left alone. Sidney turn the mind off, the little volume control. It's all manmade, no nature at all, not even a blade of grass, not even an insect, only cement and steel and glass. I don't have the energy to smash my head in. I lay on the slab of a bed and hear young Sid's saxophone, this sound filled with air, with heart. He sent me this tape with him and a bass player, it was all sweet and open, bass line and horn, so beautiful, playing these tunes that I grew up with, like "P.S I love You" and "They can't take that away from me." He's a good kid and a great saxophone player. I've been a shitty father, like my father was. Fuck, this life is full of failure and loss. I need to sleep, even in this hole, I need to sleep.

# – seventeen –

I WAKE UP AND THERE HE IS, MY KID, SIDNEY. NOT IN THE CELL, but through a glass wall with a little phone. He looks good, big and strong, a little beard, short hair, big shoulders. Jesus, I want to cry. He looks so strong and handsome. I see the fire in his eyes, like he's onto something.

"Hey dad."

"Hey Sidney, how'd you get here?"

"Plane from New York. Neeta called me. You okay?"

"Not too good."

"You burned your paintings."

"Yeah."

"Why, Dad?"

"They weren't that good. It's deadly. You didn't need to come."

Fuck, I feel the tears coming out of my eyes.

"I like the one you gave me, I've kept it with me. Pretty cool stuff. I really like it. It takes up my whole bedroom."

"You don't have to say that."

"I know I don't, it helps my music, to look at that. It's rough and random but so sweet. Neeta says you killed a guy."

"Yeah, an old wise ass rabbi."

"Why'd you do that dad."

"I don't really know, some stuff about Sammy Davis Jr. And his goddam complacency about knowing God. Sidney you didn't have to come out here."

"I know, I wanted to see you. Maybe I can help."

"How's the music going."

"Good but I can't make any money."

"I know what you mean, I wish I had some answers but I don't. You look good, strong, don't let them get you."

"Who dad."

"The system."

"Dad, can I get you anything?"

"Sid, I'd like a big fat liverwurst hero sandwich, sub, that's what they call them now. I don't know if that's allowed and yeah, a couple of babes to sleep with. I know that's not allowed. And yeah, a walkman tape player and a tape of you playing your saxophone, that would be the best. They have me, don't let them get you son. I'm sorry to do this to you, I wasn't thinking, I got sick of thinking."

"It's okay dad. I was strung out for a while, smack, you know like Bird and Sonny Rollins. But I got sick of being sick, it became not interesting. I was sick all the time and did some pretty bad stuff but never got caught. It sort of gave me a passport to the jazz underworld, the underbelly of jazz. And got to hang out and play with some pretty great players. A white Jewish junkie gains credibility, with the black genius' of jazz. You with me, dad?"

"Yeah, I love you, I'm with you."

"My girlfriend left. I did a few holdups with this cool older piano player who played great. He made a few records with Miles. No one can hear us, right?"

"I don't know. Fuck them."

"No dad, we have to be careful. So I hang with this guy and see myself in him, he's a good guy, gets eastern philosophy, has toured the world, played in Paris with Dexter and understands the complexity of music, really gets it. So we're living together in this small apartment in New York, your painting hanging on the wall, working out all these tunes, he teaches me all this stuff about chord movements on this little shitty Fender piano. Then I come home one night and he's dead, with a works in his arm. And dad, I just go to sleep, we had two rooms and a kitchen, I did that for two or three days till he started to stink, really bad. I just made believe he was sleeping, shot too much speed and had to sleep for a few days, even tried to pour water into his mouth. I finally had to call 911. I haven't gotten high since. Two years. He was a mentor, like you could be. Dad.?"

"Yeah?"

"You want mustard on the hero?"

"Yeah, but light, easy on the mustard, heavy on the tomatoes."

Some dickhead says, "Visiting hour is over."

I try to yell if he has a place to stay in LA, but some asshole leads me back to my cell. The words unheard. Jesus, what a good kid. I hope he doesn't end up like me.

I don't know when it happened or how it happened, me being like this, so damn selfish. Not being able to function in a normal way or even in a truly original way. Maybe I got some approval for a drawing I did as a kid. Maybe from some little girl or a teacher. Certainly not from my parents. Our refrigerator had no magnets. I know I got noticed for being a wise guy, an out-of-control wise guy, so I continued like all the other poor bastards in here. Wise guys with their hearts and souls broken, living like animals in a zoo. Shit, shit, shit. And the anger, Jesus, anger at the world, at the people in the world. Cruel bastards that we are, just beating on each other for no good reason or for need, if I can't get what I need in an acceptable, constructive way, I'll just take it, and this is where we end up. Did we ask for the need? No, it just consumed us. The need to be cared about, to be loved, to be held, to be talked to like human beings. The need for compassion, for some comfort. Some of us just weren't smart enough, or good looking enough, or talented enough, or lucky enough or just plain too crazy, screwed over and hurt and let down too many times. Some of us found drugs or booze or perversion or crime, to put all the need in one definable place. One neat simple package that for the moment could satisfy us or at least give us the illusion of fulfillment, which was something better than the empty hole of need that lived inside us. At least it's something. A solution.

All the jail and therapy and understanding can't change that, neither can God. He wouldn't have given us the need in first place, not the weak ones, the screwed-up ones, the ugly deformed ones. The belief can give us the illusion of comfort. But deep in our hearts, in my heart, I know it's bullshit. The truth, ugly as it is, the truth. And right now, in this cell, there's a great beauty, sardonic humor in that. The truth is the truth is the truth, on its own terms. Without our houses of worship or our inhumanity to each other. All our complicated little brain-ant circuitry can't fuck with it. On and on it goes, every advancement we make creates more destruction, us thinking, hoping we're getting someplace other than the slaughterhouse. That's not negative shit, that's the way it is. I don't have any control over these electric thoughts. Maybe because I'm locked up, incarcerated. In this orange uniform of conformity.

I've seen them out there trying to make everything right. Taking their herbal remedies, having their chiropractic adjustments, jogging, doing their workout, listening to the New Age bullshit music, watching their diets, looking out for second hand smoke, hanging out in the self-help sections of bookstores. Oh yeah, the slaughterhouse awaits them too, no matter what. No discrimination. They'd like that. You go too. Black, white, all of us. The perfect chess game where everything goes. Both Kings, both Queens, even the board goes.

I like this cell. It makes me think. So far I have no cellmate. It's only been one day but somehow time has stopped, like I've been here forever and will always be here. Before I was born and after I'm dead. A little box, corners all squared, so human and so unnatural. The obsession of manmade, this deceptive geometry, of the manmade rectangle always getting smaller.

There is no I. No Sidney with a history. No past life, no magnet-less Queens refrigerator. I hear a guy yell out from the next cell, "Let me out of here. I'm innocent, I never hurt anyone." I hear the bastards run down the hall or whatever it is, I hear them whacking him around, clubbing him, telling him to shut up. I hear the poor guy crying. Then the bastards having their little laugh, counterpointed by his moans. Poor fellow inmate whispering between the tears, "Help me, please God help me." Under my breath I say, "It's okay, they die too."

This whole place stinks. It stinks of torture and hopelessness. It stinks of unhappiness and waste and piss and shit and age and unnatural sex. That awful stench of men decaying, skin and minds rotting. It's like some bad Edward G. Robinson movie. Guys passing notes, whispering. This is fucking America, this jail. Ugly piss faced guards. We are animals in a cage. And now I want to kill, kill the society that does this to its own creatures. I can smell the sickness.

Redemption, there is no redemption. There is the fact that when they have you, they have you. And they have me. Now there's this slab of a bunk. I can't get over the anger. Big fucking deal, so we insulted your idea of how it should be. We got out of control. Big deal. Big fucking deal. The society creates its criminals, it's animals, it's addicts, making the society unavailable to the weak, the losers, the overly needy. It creates all the unnatural needs, on the tube, in the media, it's slick magazines and weekend supplements. All over the place it says, "Look what you're not!" Not young or beautiful or rich or perfect. You need this, you need that. Too bad for you, you're nothing, not clever enough, or talented enough, you're poor and stupid, no talent, no ambition. Oh you'll try to just take it. Sorry we'll have to lock you up for that. You need to get high so you don't have to think about what you don't have? Sorry we'll have to put you away for that. Punish you for not being able to satisfy the need we've shoved down your throat. Don't take it out on us, we're the good guys. You're mad at us? You want to hurt us? Well we might have to kill you for that. Yeah, well screw you all. And they say, no, screw you.

I'm exhausted. I lay down on the crappy slab of a bed and pass out.

# - eighteen -

IN THE MORNING A LETTER COMES UNDER THE DOOR. IT'S FROM Laura.

"Dear Sidney,

I didn't call the police, I don't know who did. Jaki and I and Buddy are off to the south of France for awhile. I've gotten you the best lawyer possible, please do what he says. He can work wonders, he's done it before. He'll help you beat this thing if you cooperate. I've taken the liberty of contacting your wife. It sounds like she's there for you.

It may seem too late for you but it's not. You must be empty before you can be filled, before the white light can enter you and cleanse you. I'm sure you're very close to empty. Trust me, you're at the beginning of an incredible trip. The only thing that can stop you is your anger, just let it go, allow it to exit your soul. It wants to go. Oh and Sidney, the painting we framed, the one you did with the Rabbi's blood, is hanging in a very stylish and upscale gallery in San Francisco, a museum in Paris has already put a large bid on it. I've enclosed the gallery's card. MOMA in New York has also expressed an interest. They'll hold it until you tell them what to do with it. I hope you don't mind me doing this. Sidney, everything can change in an instant, you just have to let it, be open, even in that horrible place. Your people have been through a lot and survived, so can you. We love you dear Sidney. Be brave, be open, let life enter you.

Laura, Jaki and Buddy."

The little card attached with a gold paper clip, reads, "Desire's End, San Francisco. Art of Passion."

The cell door is slammed open and a body comes flying in. The cell door is slammed shut. At first, it's just a blur. Then there he is, a young black kid on the six by eight cell floor. I can see elbows and knees bleeding. A soft voice comes out of him. "Motherfuckers, bastards, assholes. Mean pricks, I didn't do a fucking thing. Nothing!"

I go to the stainless sink and wet some toilet paper and try to wipe his bleeding elbows. He turns on his back on this ugly floor and his black bloodshot eyes look into mine. Time stops. Everything stops. This silence comes over everything. It seems like forever. Eyeball to eyeball, this forever still frame. I look at his face. Broken flat nose, top front teeth missing from his mouth, a big not quite healed scar across his black cheek, one eye swollen. The little black interior of his eyes pinned to mine. Everything stopped. The little dot in his eyes turn from fear to knowing to nothing, we hang in nothing. I put the wet rough toilet paper on his bleeding elbow, he stays still, I flush it. Then the other elbow, I can see bone, white bone. I hold the toilet paper to the open wound. He whispers, "Fuckers, dirty Motherfuckers." I somehow tell him it's going to be okay. I yell, "Guard, this man needs a doctor." Nothing. I pull him over to the toilet and put the exposed arm in and keep flushing.

Then I wrap toilet paper around his arm. He says, "Aubrey, my name is Aubrey, and thanks man. I'm in big trouble, and thanks man. I really fucked up, I'm gonna be in jail forever. I hate jail. Armed robbery, it wasn't even a real gun, finger in the pocket. I'm a junkie, my father was a junkie, my mother too, my brother too, he's dead, shot by cops, stealing a Sony in the riots. You're white, you'll go free. Hey man my arm hurts."

I get some more wet toilet paper and press it to the exposed bone. He says, "They're bad aren't they, I got no chance, do I?"

"Aubrey, I don't know anything. We got to keep your elbow clean so it doesn't get infected, okay?"

"Yeah, okay."

I put his arm in the toilet and keep flushing, to clean the wound.

"You're just a kid, right?"

"I'm seventeen and I'm bad, I've killed ugly white motherfuckers like you, at bank machines, punks taking the deposit back from corny pickup bars. They said I raped and killed a white girl jogging in the park. Now I have a girlfriend, a hot one. I'm not attracted to white chicks, they look bad to me, like corn flakes."

"I guess everyone in here is innocent."

"Yeah, except the fucking screws who kicked my black ass."

"Aubrey, we don't want your arm to get infected."

"Why do you fucking care?"

"I don't know, I really don't know. But I do care."

"I might kill you in your sleep."

"I'm not sleeping so good. But yeah, you might. I don't really give a shit, just don't fuck it up and leave me crippled or something. The bastards should sew up your elbow."

"What do they care, just another nigger, a one armed nigger, who cares? I didn't rape no white bitch. Are you a doctor?"

"No, I'm nothing, a murderer."

"No shit. That's funny, you really killed someone?"

"Yeah, a rabbi and I'm a Jew."

"That's fucked up man."

"He was Sammy Davis's rabbi."

"No shit. My father used to worship Sammy Davis. I wasn't really into him."

"Hey Aubrey, keep your arm in the toilet, it's looking pretty clean, it's a pretty deep wound. You see, you got white bones and red blood, look at that."

"You're fucking nuts, pal."

"Sid, call me Sid. I bet you're into rap."

"No, fuck that, the truth?"

"Why not?"

"I'm embarrassed about this shit."

"Yeah, so?"

"I'm into classical shit, Bach, mostly Bartok, the fucking string quartets. They're out of control, for a white motherfucker. I stole this really cool Jag when I was fourteen and that shit was on the tape deck, really cool speakers and all, surround sound, the shit just came on, I'm going, what the fuck is that. I served two years for that shit but I kept the fucking tape, Juilliard string quartet. No, fuck rap, that's some angry nigger street shit. And my friend, Sid, I'm one angry nigger but fucking Bartok was really pissed off, I'll never forget that shit and that Jag was one sweet car. I went to pick up my girlfriend, that's when I got busted. Can I take my arm out of the toilet, they're gonna kick our asses hearing this thing flushing over and over again. I'm telling you man, I'm okay. What the fuck are you doing?"

I tear up a piece of my mattress and bandage up his arm.

"I don't know what I'm doing, I guess I'm taking care of you"

"You're one old crazy motherfucker."

"That's a pretty good observation."

"You're gonna get out of here, aren't you?"

"I don't really know."

"You got money and a good lawyer, don't you?"

"They tell me I have a good lawyer. Aubrey, you okay?"

"Sure, sure man, just fucking great. I got no money, I get the fucking public defender and I'm black, African-American bullshit. I'm just another nigger who no one gives a shit about, and I'm gonna be here forever unless they kill me first."

"Where's your family?"

"Give me a break man. Who the fuck knows. You're gonna walk, aren't you?"

"I don't know."

"Oh you'll walk. Don't sweat it. Guys like you always walk or do a little time in some country club. Same old bullshit."

"Hey Aubrey, you ever hear of Auschwitz. The concentration camps, World War II. Ever hear of it?"

"I heard some things about it."

"It was no country club and nobody stole any cars or did a goddam thing. They just decided to kill us all because we were Jews. Women, little kids, all of us. This is a country club compared to that shit, you get that!"

"Okay man, chill out."

"Don't tell me to chill out!"

"Sorry man. But chill out or the screws will be on our ass. I've had enough beatings for one day, okay man?"

"Okay."

Aubrey gets on his feet. He's a tall skinny kid. He kind of shakes himself out, checks himself out to see if he's all there. He looks me over.

"What happened to your arm, Sidney?"

"It got broken twice."

He just stands there and looks at me.

"That was some low shit, that concentration camp shit."

"Yeah."

"Human beings are pretty low. I know a lot of brothers that would kill every white man on the planet if they could."

"What about the women?"

"No, they'd save their sweet white asses."

We look at each other, a smile comes to his face, first his front teeth missing, then mine, then we both crack up laughing. I take out my upper bridge and it cracks him up more. Through his laughing he says, "Sidney, you're one ugly motherfucker."

"You're no Sidney Poitier yourself."

A guard whacks his stick on the cell door. We're like a couple of kids giggling in class trying to hold it in. We hold our breath. In a whisper Aubrey says,

"I'd like to do that shit, like that guy Bartok. That is some hip shit. How'd he do that?"

"He heard it in his head and wrote it down. Then it was there forever. You want to do that?"

"Yeah, I hear shit like that, I mean sounds, like those four strings. It goes on all the time in my head. I hear them all at once, sometimes it drives me nuts. When I do junk it shuts them up for awhile."

"Aubrey listen to me, you have to learn how to write it down, I mean on music paper, it's easy."

"Fuck that, I can't even read a fucking book."

"No man it's different, it's got nothing to do with words. Shit man, we need a pencil and paper."

"You know how to do that?"

"Yeah, I took piano lessons as a kid!"

"Sidney keep your voice down."

"Here, man."

I turn over Laura's letter, no pencil, no pen. I take the bridge of my false teeth, dentures as the dentist liked to call them, I see the damp blood coming off his elbow, get a few drops of blood on the molar and draw this little red staff on the underside of Laura's note. I show him the notes, whole, quarter, half, eight, sixteenth. The scales, trying to save paper. I'm writing with my teeth on the cement floor, it all comes back, bass clef, treble clef, and Aubrey is right there with me. I go on and on, flats, sharps, key signatures, singing little scales. He gets it as fast as I can give it out. Then this horrible buzzer goes off. Aubrey tells me it's morning, we have to shower and eat breakfast. The whole floor is covered with his blood in musical notation. He's writing, making notes with my teeth, his blood. Wearing down the molar. Aubrey doesn't look well, something has changed. He has this look in his eyes of excitement, of turn-on and this look of death, the fire of death and youth.

The door slams open. A fat prick in a stupid blue uniform stands there and looks at the floor, the paper, then at us. He smiles, looks at the floor then goes towards Aubrey. "Hey nigger, look at this mess. You made a mess that you didn't clean up." I can't believe the words.

He takes his stick out and smashes Aubrey across the knees, Aubrey falls to the floor. He smashes Aubrey across the head. He looks at me and says, "Stay still, Jew bastard, you'll be out of here soon enough."

He winds up for one more swing at Aubrey's head. I grab him from behind, grab his throat and his stick and pull the stick to his throat. I feel all this power, I can feel the fat bastard dying. I smash the stick into his windpipe over and over again. At a great distance I can hear Aubrey yelling, "Don't do it! Sidney don't do it!" I feel him slip out of my hands. I take the stick and slam his head in over and over again. Fat prick laying on the floor, piss running out of him washing away the blood music lesson on the cell floor. Aubrey's eyes looking at me in disbelief. I hear all these alarms going off. I turn the ugly fat motherfucker over on his stomach and slam the stick up his ass. Through the ugly shiny blue pants.

Then they're all on me and Aubrey, beating the shit out of us. The other inmates slamming stuff around and yelling. I leap on Aubrey so I get the blows of their clubs, I protect him like a mother turtle protects her young from some crazed giant birds. I feel nothing, no pain, no fear, I hold onto Aubrey, me on his back as the clubs come down on us, like a hot rainstorm. My only need is to protect my child. I feel the blows on my spine, I feel I have this armor that nothing can penetrate. Then a terrible white and red light in my head. Falling into a deep, deep ocean, getting darker and darker, then this smiling lobster creature unable to speak, little clipping, editing movements, a thing that shreds the past, the future, everything but the moment that is, the moment of the pureness of good over evil. Then nothing. The final blow to the head, the brain. Nothing but blackness. A din of sound, voices, yelling from hell slowly fading. Gone.

# - nineteen -

NO I DON'T WANT TO WAKE AGAIN, BUT I DO. THE PAIN IS electric. I can't move anything, the pain is all over, the head first, then the chest, the arms, it centers in the knees, then the fingers, then the legs, it's my old electric train set, where it doesn't work at first and it all keeps switching, over little towns with snowflakes on the tiny trees. I look over at the other bed and it's empty, all tight and clean, I'm wrapped from head to toe and strapped down, there's some sort of plank on my arm with a needle going into it, I see a bag on a stand. There's a young blond woman standing over me, hair in a ponytail, blue eyes, dressed in white and a little sound like a metronome. There are these glass windows with wire running through them, broken sunlight coming through them. The pain is all over the place. I look at the empty bed. Where is Aubrey? I manage to say, "Where is Aubrey?" The blond nurse leaves and this guy comes in who is a cop in a suit, he has that dickhead cop look about him. I ask him where is Aubrey. He says, "Aubrey has moved on to better things, Aubrey is dead. Had a heart attack, withdrawing from crack and junk. It happens all the time." I try to move, I can't. I'm strapped down. This guy has these thin tired blue eyes. I tell him I don't want to talk. He tells me I killed a prison guard, and I'm on to the death house. Then like a tired pale gray haired Christ my lawyer appears.

"Sidney, do you know where you are?"

"In a hospital. In hell."

"You're making my job very difficult. Do you know what you did?"

"I killed the enemy, one of them, I'd like to kill them all."

"Do you want to die in the electric chair?"

"No, I want to recapture my youth, they are evil bastards who get in

STEPHEN JAY GOLDBERG

the way of truth. They should die, every last one of them. I was giving a music lesson to a friend. Is that so bad? You're a stupid motherfucker. You get little things but not the big picture." I'm having a hard time talking, I run my tongue around my mouth. Whatever teeth I had are gone, except for a few lower molars. I am a broken piece of garbage. Garbage with the ability to feel pain. With my tongue I feel these wires in my mouth, my jaw is wired together.

"The guard is quite dead. First degree murder, Sidney, that's pretty bad, in fact it's as bad as it gets."

"Let them kill me, finish the job."

"It's not really that simple, it takes years and years, that's the worst part. Years and years of abuse. Let me get you out of here."

"How in God's name can you do that?"

"I'll take care of it. You just have to cooperate and get yourself well. You think about it. I'll be back later. Sidney there's someone here to see you, your wife is here, she'd like to see you."

"Neeta?"

"Yes. Will you see her?"

"Why not."

He leaves, all I feel is this pain all over me. Everything is a blur, a fog, but I know it's goddam real. This terrible sadness comes over me. The blond nurse checks all the tubes coming in and out of me. I keep thinking, I did this, I did this to myself, to the people around me, to the world. I look at the nurse just doing her job, tending a machine, she's afraid to look at me, the killer, the lost soul. I say to her, through my wired jaw, "I wear glasses, do you know where they are?" She just goes about her business and leaves. In walks a beautiful woman in a neat blue suit, the first thing that I recognize is the scent, it's Anita. She stands over me and looks at me for a long time. She touches my hand. Then in a soft sad slow voice,

"Hello Sidney."

"Neeta, Anita, I'm sorry."

"Jesus Sidney, I can't believe what's happened, I'm sorry for you."

"You mean it?"

"Yes. At first when I saw the burnt paintings, I was so angry, so hurt, so disappointed even frightened but relieved it was over. Sidney are you okay, can you talk, can I talk to you?"

"I guess I'm not okay but please, yes, talk. Don't take your hand off mine, okay? Neeta, I screwed up really bad."

"I know you did, it's been eating you for so long, I guess it had to come to this. I never thought it would go this far. Your problems seemed so, well, I have to say it, middle class. I just had to do my own life and I thought you'd work it out, I couldn't indulge myself in your internal problems. I thought if I took care of things, you'd figure it out or just plain get sick of your self-torture."

"Well I guess being a murderer isn't so middle class, is it?"

"It's pretty bad Sidney and no, I guess it's not middle class. I always respected you and I thought the black and whites were beautiful. You want some water?"

She puts the straw in my mouth and I suck the water down.

"I did a red and white, it's in a gallery in Frisco."

"I heard all about it."

"The Museum of Modern Art wants it."

"I heard all about it. Your lawyer, Bob Eldridge, told me he'll try to get you out of this terrible trouble you're in. Sidney, I want you to come back home. If you want to. I was surprised how much I missed you."

"Anita, they killed a sweet wonderful kid, this kid Aubrey, I saw them do it and it was my fault for teaching him how to read and write music, why do they do that shit, I couldn't take it."

"Sidney, listen to me, the world isn't fair, mostly the people in it. Sid I love you, I want you to get well and come back home and paint or do whatever you want, I've stopped killing the chickens, I just eat the eggs. Sid, just do whatever Eldridge says. Okay?"

I can feel the tears running down my cheeks.

"Okay. Neeta reach under the sheet and see if I'm still there, maybe they castrated me too."

I feel her sweet hand go under the sheet and slide between my legs, I feel myself get hard. She looks at me and smiles, I smile back between the tears. Neeta is about to put her head down there when the cop enters and tells her it's time to leave. We just look at each other with soft smiles then she's gone. God, I love her.

Weeks and months go by, it seems like forever for me to heal. It looks like Laura keeps pumping the money into Eldridge, he gets me moved into a private hospital in LA. Anita is being really kind and understanding. She rented a house in LA with my son Sidney and his girlfriend. It turns out I'm broken really bad, legs, arms, skull. The blows to the head caused a tumor or clot or something bad. They do some surgery and I turn out okay. It takes two years before I'm well enough to go to trial. I have all this time to think. I just lay there most of the time and think, more like watch myself think. Two years is a long time to think. And the cops are still around all the time, I'm still legally in jail, but Eldridge keeps working wonders. Anita comes to visit and we have this hot sneaky sex. She comes to see me all dressed up but with no underwear on, we play all these games that remove the pain. This physical healing has forced my mind to change. I can't but think this situation I committed myself to has changed her outlook. I think the rabbi had to die, the guard had to die but not dear Aubrey, that was pure evil.

I realize again that the world of the human species is evil, desperate. Stuck in this hospital I read all the books on humanity, on philosophy, psychology. I get fascinated by the insect world, the plant world, the cosmic world. I can't get high, here in this bed, except for the pain killers, which don't do much. Neeta keeps them coming, the books. Somehow the immobility that the terrible beating has caused has forced me to research the truth. I have this bookstand on my bed because my arms get tired from holding them. We talk one to one, me and the minds: Freud, Einstein, Krishnamurti, Buddha, Jung, Christ, Moses, the list would take up volumes, and the great novelists and the artists. Books. It's all there, every mind that came before me. Every thought in the silence of words. The written word. Now all I want to do is live and get it. There is such a huge history of humanity trying to get it. Galileo, Darwin, Michelangelo, DaVinci, Plato. Hundreds, thousands every man and woman that has ever lived wants to get it. The genius musicians, I want to hear and see it all. The access is beyond belief. The search for answers. That is the exciting goodness of the human mind, the human soul. To learn, to find the evasive truth and to be able to express it, so we all get it. I'm sure the truth is out there on its own terms. It has given us, man-woman this beautiful struggle to connect, to lock in, to take off into this vision of the real.

I remember as a kid, killing an ant on the sidewalk. I knew it was important. It was walking along then dead, crushed. I couldn't sleep that night, thinking about it. I was ten. I thought it was not important because it was small. Then my father took me fishing, these were bigger creatures. I had to clean the fish in the backyard. Cut out their guts, scale them, cut off their heads while swatting files off my arms, them falling dead. This switch that we had control of over lesser creatures. That's what they did to Aubrey, turned his switch off. A lesser creature and they let me live.

I know the truth isn't in any book or ritual or any teaching. Yeah, maybe little pieces that give some kind of comfort. I've seen it with the guys in prison or the dying here in the hospital, the praying, the God please help me, kind of stuff. I've felt it in that timeless feeling. I don't really think the mind can ever get it because the mind is part of it. The embodiment of the

STEPHEN JAY GOLDBERG

confusion and the desperation. I don't know what makes me do things or not do things, so much of it just seems to happen, taking actions. That kid, Aubrey, really did something to me, for me. I wanted so much to give him something and he so was able to receive. That was new for me. I can only imagine the crap he survived. Those bastards beat him to death, like they've been doing through the ages, like we've been doing through the ages. Like me with the ant at ten years old.

My body continues to heal. I don't know why but it does it on it's own. I remember the day they took the wires out of my jaw and the day I was able to sit up, then move to a chair and go to the bathroom with a walker. I guess they can't execute a man who's too sick to die.

At the arraignment Eldridge had me plead not guilty for killing the guard. I appeared in court with a walker and they had me handcuffed to it, with shackles on my feet, as if I could escape. The prosecutor offered a plea bargain of ten to twenty for manslaughter. Bob said screw that, it was self-defense and I was trying to protect another inmate. The cool thing was Eldridge got this long history of inmate abuse about this prick. John Hargy was his name. He was even busted for child pornography and beating up his ex-wife. He was once brought up on charges of sexually abusing his kids, which he walked on. I'm so glad the California Department of Corrections has such high standards. The state prosecutor offers a better deal, no jail, two years probation. Eldridge tells him to forget it. Then the stuff comes out in the LA Times and it's a big deal, all over TV and all. There's all this stuff in the media about abuse in prison. Eldridge tells me we don't talk to anybody. I keep telling him about how they killed Aubrey. He tells me to forget it, he's gone, we can't help him. Then one day he walks into my hospital room with this old black woman. He says, "This is Aubrey Willson's grandmother. I told her what you did, trying to save him."

She thanks me. She says,

"Aubrey was a good a boy, he lost his mom, my baby girl, real young."

I can't say anything.

"So I hope everything works out for you. I heard you took a bad beating trying to save him. You're a good man. Thank you for trying. I'll pray for you. Jesus died on the cross for that boy."

I take her hand and hold it, then the time stop thing happens, eyes to eyes. She looks at me as if to ask if it's okay, and then gives me this soft electric kiss on my forehead. She says,

"Young man, tell me your name again."

"Sidney."

"Yes, Sidney. Sidney, these things happen for a reason. I have a lot of faith in the goodness of the human soul. My people have had a hard time, so have your people, that makes a bond between us. I'm eighty-nine years old, I can't count all my grandchildren or great grandchildren, there's a bundle of them. Lots of them are dead, I've been to so many funerals. I don't know why I go on, I guess the Lord wants me to. Maybe to be here in this moment to comfort you. Doing bad things doesn't make you bad. I told Aubrey that. He was a good boy. So thank you for trying to save him. He's off to a better place. Thank you, I wanted to meet you, thank you. Jesus loves you."

Then she's gone. Eldridge walks her out.

I lay there, seeing an after-image of her, like she's still in the room. I don't want to be touched or moved into some sentimental crap about the "Goodness of the human soul." But something in me wants to give up, let it go, like a fighter who's too exhausted to move his arms. The beautiful old lady lays the final punch on me. I say it out loud, "What does it take to surrender?"

# - twenty -

I GET OUT OF BED, PICK UP THE WALKER. THEY HAVE ME ON the second floor of this civilian hospital. I smash the walker through the window and jump out through the broken glass, my knees hit grass. I'm in the parking lot, near the emergency room. There's a car with the headlights on and the door open, next to the emergency room entrance. There's blood on the passenger seat. The keys on the floor under the steering wheel. I get in, insert the key, turn it and I am off. The radio is on, it's a talk show, a woman's voice says, "I have two million dollars in the money market and fifty thousand in my checking account, I'm concerned that the fifty thousand is not earning interest. Bruce, what's your advice?" This fat voice says. "That's too much in checking, you're losing interest, how old are you?" The woman's voice answers, "Seventy-six, and Bruce, I'm a widow." Bruce tells her not to worry she'll never be poor and to try to have some fun. She asks, "Bruce, at my age? Fun?" He says; "Sweetheart, take a cruise, go to Las Vegas, join a senior singles group. Enjoy honey."

There's blood on the passenger seat, still wet and warm as my hand rests on the upholstery. A commercial comes on. Something about life extending vitamins. I'm in this hospital gown, driving, again driving in the dark on interior roads. I look at the fuel level, next to full. There's a woman's handbag on the passenger floor, nice soft leather. I'm in the city, LA all closed down for the night. I take out a perfumed silk handkerchief and give it a sniff, not too bad. I want to see signs that say East. I want to go home.

This car is automatic, pretty new, a Taurus or something. I can't find a damn freeway. I'm in some creepy neighborhood, people hanging out on the street. I stop at a light. A young black guy comes over and says,

"Crack?" I punch the gas, through the red light. I zip up the electric windows and find the AC. Another light. It's a hooker corner, a young blond white babe in a mini skirt knocks on the window and smiles. I stop at the light and find the window button. She says, "Twenty bucks, five minutes, blow job, hand job ten." I open up the handbag. I spot a fifty and a bunch of other bills. I tell her, "Get in."

I ask, "What's your name?"

"Just call me Honey, that's because I'm sweet. Jesus, mister, what are you wearing?"

"Just a little something to make it easy for you."

"It looks like hospital garb."

"Yeah Honey, I'm ready for anything."

"Why don't you pull into that parking lot, it's cool, we pay them off, it's safe."

She pulls down her black tube top and has these nice firm young breasts. I tell her I'd rather keep moving. I manage to get a twenty out of the leather bag and give it to her. She puts her head down on my lap and gets to work. Nothing like a pro. I'm glad it's an automatic, no stick in the way. It is over pretty quick. I circle around the block and drop her where I picked her up. She says getting out of the car; "Nice touch with the hospital gown." Take care Honey. The whole night world looks a little clearer, so does my situation.

I slow down and try to think. If I keep driving, I'll get caught sooner or later. Where am I going? Mexico? Back to New York? Jesus, I don't know. My right knee is all swollen, starting to throb. Amazing how pleasure can overcome pain, at least for the moment. I click the radio back on. A guy is saying how he owes over twenty grand on his credit cards, how his wife doesn't know about it, he's lost his job an has a second mortgage out on his house and needs some advice. Bruce tells him to cut up his cards, get any two or three jobs he can and work out a payment plan. Then he tells him, good luck guy. What would Bruce tell me?

I find myself right back at the emergency room. The damn car like a homing pigeon. I leave the car right where I found it, take a sniff of the silk handkerchief and limp into the ER. This admitting nurse looks at me with all this fear in her eyes. I tell her I fell out the damn window, trying to go to the bathroom. All these cops don't know what to do. Before I know it, I'm back in my room, plastic over the broken window. There's two stupid cops in the room looking at me, with that stupid, "I'm in charge" look on their faces, a nurse putting an ice pack on my knee, about sixteen inches lower than Honey's little visit. I see a little smile on her face, like she knows something the cops don't, maybe something I don't know. I miss the Bruce guy on the radio. I'll ask Neeta to get me a little radio.

Now I never thought about myself as lucky, mostly the opposite. The only lucky thing about me I'm pretty good looking. Even at this age, tall, thin, full head of now gray hair. Sort of a jewish Cary Grant. In fact I don't do a bad English accent. I read somewhere that they did a study of mental patients and the better-looking ones got better quicker because they get more attention. I doesn't seem very fair, but what is?

The next day in comes Eldridge, all business. Like he has some kind of news, Anita is with him. They make a pretty nice couple. I wonder if lawyers get to make it with the women they represent in divorce cases. I bet they do. Neeta should have married a guy like Eldridge and once in a while screwed around with artist types. A hard-working guy like Eldridge is probably never home and brings in big dollars.

"Well Sidney, I have some news for you. I met with the state's attorney. He has no case, he knows it and so do I. You understand. You're a free man, no trial, no nothing. Six months probation and that's it. It's over. Your little ride last night didn't help. I want to show you something."

A woman in business suit comes in to the hospital room pushing a huge hand truck filled with boxes.

"That's your paperwork. Thank you Linda. And you my friend, can thank Laura. She spent a lot of money on this case."

I look at Neeta, then at the ceiling.

"Thank you Laura."

"Sign here Sidney. You don't need to read it. Believe me."

"What am I signing?"

Neeta says, "For Christ's sakes Sid, sign it."

"It says you're guilty of DUI number one, okay?"

"Okay." I sign the damn thing.

Eldridge looks at the two dopey cops, they leave without tripping over each other.

# — twenty-one —

THE BLOND NURSE WHEELS ME OUT INTO THE SMOGGY LA sunlight. Neeta by my side, young Sidney by the waiting cab looking all smiles with his saxophone case. There's even a few photographers. A reporter comes over and asks me something I don't hear.

"Listen, those bastards killed an innocent kid who could have been a great composer. They should lock up all the guards and let out all the poor bastards in the joint and give them some help and some money and some care. The penal system stinks. It's run by some sadistic, underpaid idiots. And…"

Neeta grabs my hand and pulls me into the cab.

First the airport, young Sidney says he's got some gigs in LA and heads off. Neeta and I board the plane to Kennedy. While we're on the plane we get the news about the Kennedy kid crashing his plane off Martha's Vineyard with his wife and her sister. The beautiful people die too, a little turn of the wheel, a miscalculation. The whole population in mourning. I want to get up on my seat and tell them about Aubrey and I'm sure thousands of others like him. I want to tell them about Aubrey's beautiful grandmother and her timeless eyes, and her forever mourning her losses, to poverty and the drugs of escape. The handsome Kennedy kid's face flashes on the sky screen, where is Aubrey's beautiful face with the pigs beating his head in? Where's the guy with the lethal injection in his arm and the seafood dinner in his stomach? The Kennedy kid is beautiful, handsome but so are they.

We land at Kennedy at dawn, there's a Subaru tuna-can in the outer lot. I say to Neeta, "I got rid of that thing," and she says, "I bought another one, same model, color and year." Neeta drives, I hit the radio, no Bruce,

I leave it to classical, real soft. We haven't spoken since we left LA, except to order dinner and drinks.

"You really want me back?"

"Yes."

"Why?"

"You're my husband."

"You care about me? You give a damn?"

"I do, yes."

"I'm not much good."

"I know."

Then this string stuff comes on the classical station, it's the Bartok String Quartets. I imagine Aubrey in his stolen Jag hearing this for the first time, like I'm hearing it. We're going over the Triborough Bridge, Neeta wearing her driving glasses. I put my head down on her lap and listen to the confusing intense counterpoint, as I smell the sweet smell between her thighs. Looking up at her face, I don't know her, like I didn't know Honey or Laura or anything. The stars show through the inverted windshield, distorted by the curvature of the glass. I reach up and kiss her sweet soft mouth. I can't believe she's taking me home. She's wearing a dress, soft cotton, I feel her calf through the pantyhose. It makes me think she fucked Eldridge, she never wore pantyhose. I keep thinking how perfect they looked together. It makes me hot, her being hot with another man. Anita and a killer lawyer. I look up at the night sky through the windshield, my head on Neeta's lap. I slide my hand between her legs and feel her wetness through the pantyhose as she drives on.

I hear Neeta's soft voice,

"I have a surprise for you."

The house where we lived is embers, black, nothing, burnt down.

"It's gone, all of it, nothing Sid, gone, past. I burned it all. Only land and sky, ninety-five acres of nothing but nature."

Now I want to sleep in a clean house, between clean sheets, with a bath and a kitchen.

"It's gone Sid, isn't that beautiful. Get out of the car. Come here babe, take my hand."

Neeta takes a gas can and empties it on the Subaru, puts a match to it and up it goes. She pulls me away and it blows up, gone. Then she leads me up over this hill and there it stands, it looks like light, only light. "Come on babe." I hear a dog barking, it's Buddy the smiling dog. Neeta's pulling me towards the light.

"We can start over Sid, we're not too old, we're not dead, not yet."

Neeta lays me down onto the soft grass. There's no moon, only stars.

We look up, lying on our backs, the stars glittering.

"Sid, I don't understand anything. I've tried, I really have. I've had this time to myself, the time I've always wanted. I don't know why I wanted it, maybe to get to know myself. For a while I was so very glad you were gone. I really thought you were the problem, this thing eating away at me, I was so sure it was you. You invading me. You the troubled one. Me always okay. Look at that!" A shooting star crosses the night sky.

"I'm confused about values, a guy came over to fix the furnace, he was young and a hard worker. I had sex with him. It was distant, like the sky, so far away from me. He came by the next day telling me how he wanted to leave his wife and be with me. I felt bad about invading his life, he had two small kids, he told me how dull his life was, how unsexy it was and how hard he worked. He tried to have sex with me again. I was afraid, he was drunk and so unhappy. He grabbed me and ripped off my clothes, I was sure he was going to kill me, he looked so ugly, so full of fear. Sid, I let him do it, I just lay there and knew I was coming back to you. After, he slammed the screen door and drove off in his red pick-up. There was nothing hot or interesting about it. Sid, are you here?"

"I'm here."

Then this thing happens in the sky, the northern lights, the whole sky goes into this ripple of colors, this curtain of light, shimmering. My eyes open wide. Neeta gets close to me, on top of me. I hold her hair and look to the sky. She rubs on me through our clothes, little soft sounds.

"Sidney, I can't believe you killed someone."

"I did baby, I did, there are some real shits in this world."

"Do you want to kill me?" She rubs on me harder.

"No, you're a good girl."

"You think so?"

"I know so."

"Sid, you're the only one that can make me come. Why is that?"

"I haven't the faintest idea."

"I have a big surprise for you baby."

Anita on top of me, her eyes wide open, looking down at me, all fire, all alive, pressing and rubbing, the sky going nuts, she just keeps saying,

"We survive, we survive, honey we survive, no matter what. Don't we. Don't we!"

Her voice running circles around the stars.

One last, "Don't we?" She comes through everything, her soft cotton dress all wet, her sweet breath in my ear.

We fall asleep under the night sky.

We wake in the warm sunlight, holding hands we walk over a small hill, there's a new A-frame structure, new pine boards, glass skylights. Under old maple trees. I fall in the leaves, unable to comprehend. She says,

"Doing bad things doesn't make you bad."

We enter the new building, there are hundreds of stretched canvases leaned against a stone wall.

"He built it for you, the guy I fucked, is that okay? Sidney? He said, this guy of yours must be something special. Sidney? Sidney no more, okay? No more blame, I love you babe."

Daylight is pouring in, I see every part of Neeta's body, every wrinkle, each tiny hair on her perfect frame, everything about her magnified, I see each year of her aging, see her as an old woman watching spiders on the wall. Her eyes still young.

"Sidney we're going to be okay. Please tell me that, please? I can't do anymore."

"We are going to be okay."

"Did you ever notice if you say a word over and over and over it loses any meaning."

"Neeta?"

"What."

"We might not be okay."

"I know. Sid?"

"Yeah?"

"No more talking."

"Good idea."

— end —

John **BUTLER,** dear friend, quite brilliant, I met him in a place of recovery, we helped each other. He was up here in Vermont in a halfway house. A kind, interesting man. We connected in a big way. Same sarcastic New York sense of humor, same struggle with addiction. He was kind and smart and really funny with a huge heart.

John would do things like write bad checks and steal stuff in department stores. What he bought he would keep, then put rags or old socks or underwear in the plastic package and reseal it, he had a machine that did that, then return the resealed package and get his money back. He was also a talented shoplifter. A small time criminal who never hurt anybody but himself.

We tried to get sober together. I had about three months, holding on by my fingernails, he had about nine months. One night he called, I could tell by the "hello" he was stoned and happy, when we hung up I poured myself a drink. And so it goes.

He bought or stole my young daughter these beautiful Georgia O'Keefe prints that still hang on her wall. He would sing old songs to her, with a George Burns delivery. He didn't make it, never had any kids, never had a real home or family, or as far as I know a loving lover. His lover was drugs and alcohol.

One time i got this job recording some sort of conference. Really boring stuff. It paid pretty well but I didn't quite have the equipment, two double cassette recorders. John had this idea. We went to Service Merchandise and I bought the two recorders, did the recordings and made the required copies. Then returned the recorders to Service Merchandise so I could get my money back. We had a good time and many laughs. And we did get paid well.

The last time he called from Atlanta he said his liver was gone. He was medium drunk. He was making all this money working and stealing in a porno shop. He bought a house in Atlanta that he filled with hookers, crack and booze. He told me crack was the worse addiction ever. I never messed with it.

He had driven cabs in New York City with a fake drivers license. In his youth John would steal cars in New York and sell them in Vermont. He could have been a great writer or filmmaker, but found small time crime and getting high far more interesting.

He sort of looked like and sounded like the actor who played Woody Allen's best friend in Annie Hall. He would tell me interesting books to read and unknown films to see and he loved jazz.

I miss him. A complicated human being. He was a really good friend, sober or stoned. I haven't heard from John in over five years so I know he's dead. Hey John. Rest in peace, at last, in some unmarked grave, as if the marks matter. I was glad to know you and laugh with you. Be true friends.

I miss you buddy, but I get it, your life style and fuckups. Good dear friend.

## I REALLY DO GET IT.

Love, Steve

# First night in
# barbados

it had been a
long
plane trip
from
New York
arriving at
night

dressed in a
suit
my horn
a suitcase
where to go

a cab to
Bridgetown
looking for
live music
and mount gay
rum

I found it
could hear
the music from
the street
below

was it jazz or
calypso
no matter
went up
drank some rum

uncased my horn
played with the band
then drinks were free
hugs and smiles

the owner/bartender
name was Slims
I told him
interesting to have a plural
name

more free drinks
and smiles

I'm in my twenties
got hired to play
at the Barbados Hilton

as it got later and later
the band packing up
club emptying out
me at the bar

I realized I had no
place to stay
no hotel
no bed

a nice looking
dark woman
sitting next to me
at the bar
asked if
I'd like to come
home with her
nice smile

I asked how much
she said
five dollars for the night
not a bad deal

she walked me
through a funky
dark part of Bridgetown
so very strange to me

we got to her almost house
me so tired
with suitcase and horn
no fear at all

we had sex
her skin felt
new and smooth
in the almost house

had the scent of
interesting
people sleeping
old and young

I had a deep sleep
in the morning
there were chickens
in the room

a small boy child
having a piss
in the corner

I gave her a soft kiss
in the blinding sunlit
morning not sure
where I was
I got dressed

suit and all
picked up my
not stolen
horn and suitcase

walking outside
wrinkled suit
the neighborhood kids
laughing and smiling

me being someplace
I should not have been
with a horn case
and a suitcase

I did smile back
never one bit of fear
being exactly where
I didn't belong

young and strong

the woman
was okay
we had a good sleep
and a good fuck

she was asleep
when I left
I hope I kissed her
goodbye

a tender five bucks
first night
in Barbados

# IDIOT tears

i hate arrogant pricks
who know how to spell
and think they have it all together

there is no such thing as
all together, we're all fucked
so get comfortable with it

if you're 14 or 85
it never gets
together
just habits and the illusion of comfort

all make believe
to make believe in illusion
and i don't give a fuck
how much I use the word
illusion or fuck

i'm a fuckin' failure
and long for death
as much as a dying man
longs for life

the truly important thing
is no one gives a fuck
mostly myself

**listen to me**
**in the end no one really gives a fuck**

STEPHEN JAY GOLDBERG

190

okay, okay, okay
when she died
and I held her in death
through the night
half drunk, half sane

and the asshole hopeless workers
said let go, she'll start to smell
the death rotting smell
i told them to fuck off

i just wanted to keep her warm
and never let her go
i knew she wasn't breathing
and had no heart beat
but she had a body
that i could hold and
try to keep warm

nothing like it
death
it's almost like fucking
in it's passion

they came in the morning
men in dark suits
and took her into the fire

came back the the next morning
with a blue box
with her ashes

I wanted to kill them
kill every thing
a fucking blue box

when i looked in
the ashes that were so white
i thought ashes were black
in a fuckin plastic bag
in the blue box
her name written on top

i don't much care about anything
and have no belief system
and work every day
at the no belief and slow
sensual suicide

and can't wait to get the cancer
and feel the pain waiting for death
so I can share it with her
except i'll be fuckin alone

**with a pistol in my mouth**
**or a bottle of pills**
**or both**

i am really tired, really tired
and hope i don't wake
with the dull hangover
and idiot wet tears
that's how the best of love goes

STEPHEN JAY GOLDBERG

192

# CROAK notes

MOST OF THEM ARE croaked, FRIENDS, LOVERS, HEROES, croaked
DONE FOREVER, SIMPLE WORD: DEAD
I LIKE croaked BETTER, SORT OF FROG-LIKE
I'VE MADE A LIST OF THEM, IT'S PRETTY LONG
I WON'T GO THROUGH IT, BUT THEY ARE THERE
NOT HERE AND I MISS THEM
BUT FUCK THAT

SO I TOLD JANET I DIDN'T LIKE MY COCK
THIS WAS A LONG TIME AGO
I'M BAD AT YEARS
SHE HAD LONG RED HAIR
AND COULD DRINK WITH ME ALL NIGHT
THEN GET UP FOR WORK AT EIGHT AM

WHEN I TOLD HER THAT
SHE SLAMMED ME ON HER BED
IN HER SWEET VILLAGE GARDEN APARTMENT
SHE STRIPPED ME AND TIED ME UP
AND WENT DOWN ON ME AS SHE POURED
A DRINK INTO MY MOUTH
AND GOT ME REAL HARD, DRUNK AS WE WERE

SHE SAID, I CAN HEAR HER AND SEE HER
"YOU DON'T LIKE THIS COCK, I FUCKIN LOVE IT"
SHE GOT ON TOP, I COULDN'T MOVE
BUT FELT THIS HAPPINESS AND LAUGHTER

GOD SHE WAS BEAUTIFUL

A PSYCHIATRIC SOCIAL WORKER
AFTER SHE UNTIED ME
WE HAD CAVIAR AND CREAM CHEESE
ON RITZ CRACKERS, WITH MORE DRINKS
AND HAD THESE GREAT INTERESTING CONVERSATIONS

THEN SHE'D GET THE NEEDLE OUT
WE'D SHOOT EACH OTHER UP WITH VITAMIN B12
RIGHT IN THE ASS, HER BEAUTIFUL ASS
IN HER BEAUTIFUL PLACE OFF SHERIDAN SQUARE
THE ANTI-HANGOVER HIT

WHEN I WOKE SHE WAS GONE
OFF TO HELP THE LESS FORTUNATE
BREAKFAST WAS ON THE TABLE
I'D WALK AROUND GREENWICH VILLAGE
MEETING FRIENDS, PLAY SOME CHESS
WATCH THE GENIUS CHESS PLAYERS
IN WASHINGTON SQUARE PARK, FLIRT WITH SOME BABES

THEN BACK TO JANET, SO INTERESTING
WITH FRESH BOOZE AND CIGARETTES
SHORT TALKS ABOUT HER CLIENTS
FUCKED UP PEOPLE AND WE WERE GOOD

LOVING, FUN, DELICATE FOOD, NEVER DINNERS
"SO YOU DON'T LIKE YOUR COCK, I FUCKIN LOVE IT"
THEN THE SCREAMING TIED UP SEX
AND THE ANTI-HUNG-OVER INJECTIONS, SO SEXY

THEN THE NIGHT I FUCKED IT ALL UP
PLAYING IN THIS COOL JAZZ CLUB
AND THIS ASSHOLE TAKES ME INTO
THE BATHROOM AND LAYS OUT
ALL THESE LINES OF COCAINE ON HIS FOREARM
GAVE ME A ROLLED UP BILL AND I DO THEM
ALL THE LINES AND I STILL WANT MORE
COKE IS LIKE THAT

THE PLACE CLOSES, IT'S 4 AM
I CALL SWEET JANET AND SAY
I'LL BE RIGHT THERE, I CAN TELL SHE'S SOUND ASLEEP

I BRING THIS JERK OVER, JANET IN HER NIGHTGOWN
AND HE'S LOOKING AT HER
IN A WAY I DON'T LIKE
WE DO A FEW MORE LINES, COKE IS LIKE THAT

I TELL HIM IT'S TIME TO LEAVE
HE PULLS THIS GUN,
I'M REALLY FEELING GOOD
JANET JUST WANTS TO SLEEP

THEN I DO THIS STRANGE THING
I SMASH THE GUY IN THE FACE AND TAKE HIS PIECE
TELL HIM TO GET THE FUCK OUT

HE LEAVES, I GET IN BED WITH BEAUTIFUL JANET
THINGS WERE NEVER THE SAME

I DON'T KNOW WHERE SHE IS
**croaked** OR NOT **croaked**
A LONG TIME AGO
I HOPE SHE KNOWS
I'M THINKING ABOUT HER TONIGHT
I HOPE SHE HAS MEMORIES OF ME

# WOMAN

## FROM
# Amsterdam

You see
all gone
I hate fuckin lessons
of intelligent ways to live

**I knew a woman from amsterdam**
that said things
that made me secure in my aspect of giving
her husband sat on my lap
wearing a wig showing me a book
of the canals of holland
while she built a fire
in a rare new york city fireplace

and this perfect gentleman
knew I was drunk
and fucking his wife
as if his UN delegation
had an effect
as strong as the attraction
his wife and I had together

he showed me the canals
as if I were some schmuck
who had never sucked
his wife's sweet nipples
as if I had no internal canals
internal unpolluted canals

I can never forget the way she came
down the stairs
me trying so hard to focus
on the meaningless book
and the charm of the accent
I would not have been surprised
if she sucked him off in the
elegant bathroom
just to give him permission
to leave

then the lecture she gave me
about honesty and truth
about sex and tai chi
about high and clearness
spun my head with no slap

the enjoyment of the memory
has no enjoyment
the shitty serpent of memory
the brain memory
is just a pain
in a body lost

# My X - RAY Angel

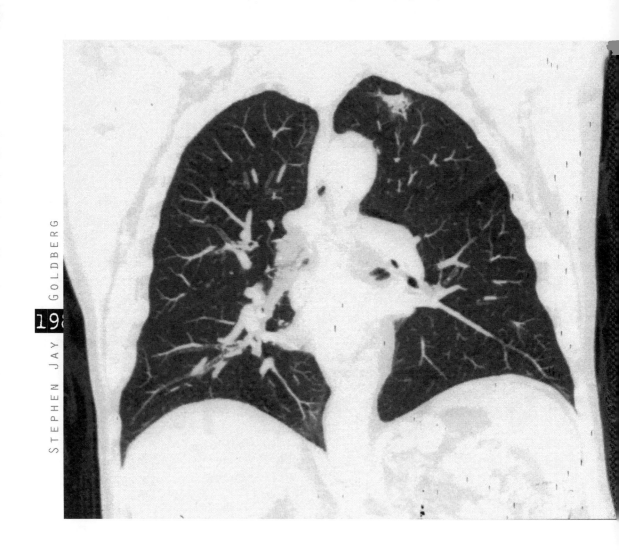

198

# one of My Biggest fuck ups

I was sitting in with **David Amram** in a
little club in Greenwich Village.

David was playing piano, he also played French horn
and was the assistant conductor under **Leonard Bernstein**
in the New York philharmonic. **Mingus** was in the house.

After I payed **Charles Mingus** invited me to sit down with him
and I think maybe he bought me a drink.
He said, (no shit), *"I like the way you play."*
Me being a bit drunk *young and arrogant*
Said, *"So why don't you give me a gig with your band?"*

**He** said, "I'm doing a concert at the **Filmore East** next weekend.
*you be there,* play in my band. No, **no rehearsals."**
I was pretty flipped out. **a concert with Mingus** in my
twenties.

So Saturday night **I get dressed pretty cool**
**after practicing all week.**
I head down to the Fillmore, I get there early.
The place looks kind of dark.
I tell the woman in the box office,
*I'm here to play the Mingus concert.*
She says, **"That was last night !"**

# Dog night

the dog is blind
her belly is swollen
some sort of liver deal
she doesn't drink

she is not my dog
but when she knows i'm there
it makes her happy
her tail wags and she goes nuts
when I come in the door

she is not my dog
but a dear friend's dog

i'm very lonely, but i don't want a dog
i can't take care of myself
nor does anyone else

i could not pick up dog shit
put it in a plastic bag
and ask the garbage people to take it away

i desperately need unconditional love
i had it, i know it
it was taken away in a bag
that I refused to watch
returned in a blue box with white ashes
inside the box the ashes were in a plastic bag

I'VE HAD DOGS IN MY LIFE
LADDY, BUZZY, MAXWELL, SHERLOCK

STEPHEN JAY GOLDBERG

200

I'VE HAD WIVES IN MY LIFE
RENEE, HOLLY, HARRIET, RACHEL
TROPICAL FISH AND GOLD FISH

children in my life
jonas, matt, emma
grandchildren liam and ava

lovers that i remember and don't remember
don't know if they remember me
or if they are dead or alive
we had great fun and sex
so now i'm tired
yet can slam a tennis ball
lift weights, play a horn
pump hard on a bike

my teeth are gone, a fair deal
my mind is going, a fair deal
after all the loving alcohol
my friend who never fails
to shut up the pain part
of the brain and heart

today i so much wanted to die
get this shit over with
at this late stage of the game

THREE BEAUTIFUL WOMEN SAVED ME
FIRST JEANEE, WITH HER DISTANT
UNDERSTANDING
INGER, WITH HER SOFT TOUCH
AND AMY THE BLIND DOG,
WITH HER HAPPINESS TO KNOW I WAS THERE
HAPPY TAIL WAGGING

in her life, she doesn't know she's blind
or has a swollen liver
all she knows is she doesn't want
to be alone, she climbs the stairs
and sleeps at the foot of the bed

not really knowing she is not with her own kind

as i don't know if i'm with my own kind

BUT I ACCEPT THE NEEDY COMFORT
THE WARM BODY, AND THE NICE BREAKFAST
THE BLIND LOVING DOG, THE WARM LOVING
ALCOHOL

and the backwards dreams lost
of every wrong turn

STEPHEN JAY GOLDBERG

# Important

I don't know
I don't know

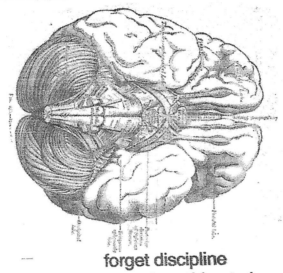

forget discipline
there is nothing to learn
that you don't already know

Banas
Decafe
Soda
English Mu
Red pepper
Spinach
Canned Ch.

# Malcom LEIGH

WE WERE FRIENDS IN THE VILLAGE DAYS
BROUGHT TOGETHER BY THE TRUMPET
AND OUR LOVE OF WOMEN

MAL PLAYED THE TRUMPET
COULDN'T REALLY IMPROVISE
HAD A NICE TONE
WANTED TO BE A
HIGH NOTE PLAYER

HE HAD A SMALL APARTMENT
IN THE VILLAGE

WE'D GO DOWN
TO THE HUDSON RIVER
AND DO THE MAGGIO SYSTEM
TOGETHER

A LONG ARPEGGIO TRUMPET
EXERCISE
TO DEVELOP HIGH NOTES
IT WAS A GOOD WORKOUT

*WE WERE YOUNG*
*GOOD FRIENDS*

MAL WORKED IN A RECORD STORE
COLONY RECORDS ON SEVENTH AVENUE

ONE DAY I SAID TO HIM
YOU HOLD THE HORN
IN A STRANGE WAY
YOUR LEFT HAND

HE SAID
YOU NEVER NOTICED

NOTICED WHAT

MY LEFT ARM DOESN'T WORK
POLIO AS A KID

I NEVER NOTICED

*HE WAS A GOOD GUY*

# HOW *Could* HE

every poem is a love poem to you
every song is a love song to you

it's the hole in my heart
that keeps me alive
next to the thoughts of suicide

death ate you
you filled him too full
to devour me

he must be spinning
to have you inside him
he must love you so much

he killed you so slowly
piece by piece

invaded your breast
your lungs, your brain
little spots on the cat scan
then your heart gently stopped

so many months of foreplay
the way he took you
away from me

death loved you so much
in places I couldn't touch

I couldn't compete
with the rage in his eyes
he couldn't take me

death so jealous
he had to have you
get you away from me

the way he loved you
and tore you apart
his form of tenderness
his need for greed

quiet monster
un-fightable devil
I know he's laughing at me
my broken heart
how he loves to see
me alone
broken in tears

he says, what do you want
I gave you 25 years
enjoy your martini
and cigarette
I have her now
for eternity
you can't have her back
she's my wife now
my wife now

sorry I can't take you
I'm too in love

I don't like you
or the passion you had

she told me all about it
with tears in her eyes
I'm her lover now
she has no choice

no, I won't take you
I worship her

you can drive fast
with eyes closed
in a whiteout or blackout
needle in your arm
you can't OD

I don't want you here
you'll take her away from me

I'm death and I'm scared
that you'll get her back
I love her so much
I don't want you here

I had to kill her
that's what love does

you'll get here someday
and have her back

my heart will be broken
I'll just kill more
maybe another holocaust

I'm death
I don't want you around
to see you together
and make love again

I'm in love with her
I don't want you around
she still loves you
in this outside world

your death will be sudden
a twisted knife
I'll make her watch
and again
she'll be your wife

I'll blow up the earth
tear out the stars
I'll kill you all

I love her so much

I'll kill you all

I'm death
I love her so much
I'll kill you all

# Catalina

her name was **catalina**
there was no exchange of fluids

she was tall and striking
always in flowing white
past the age of
perfect youth

fearless in her aloneness
such sophisticated poverty
gentle smile and humor
fearless in her aloneness

two tiny white dogs
helper dogs she called them
they ate only raw food
raw animal meat
raw chickens
**she made headdresses out of**
**the chicken feathers**

she must have been
such a beauty
still was at sixty
her skin
was beginning to hang
on her body

had been a celibate nun
could have been a movie star
homeless in san pancho, mexico
walked the beach at sunrise
and sunset

loved smoking pot
candles and feathers
always in a kind way
**asking for a cigarette**
**them always looking**
**so sophisticated in her mouth**

an ancient free spirit
more into giving than taking
in flowing white

me thinking it was so sad
her so past sex
it was the sunrise
and the burning sunsets
the two dog accessories
and walks on the
mexican beaches that interested her
or didn't interest her

i've always loved
intelligent, mystical women
and had an interest in what they ate
or refused to eat

she had offered me
a raw chicken meatball
i refused
**she offered me**
**a sculpture made of**
**a pelican head**
i couldn't pack it

last i heard
she was so thin
walking the mexican beaches
a bit sick

knowing her
she accepts sickness
like the power of the san pancho waves
yes we had an attraction
but she was too old
beaten by time

catalina made it clear
that she was past sex
like the seas undertow
her tall body
in white flowing clothes
with the double dogs
and fading body
and great intelligence

i could have seduced her
we both knew that
it would have been
an insult to her purity
and her brilliant poverty
we knew how to laugh about it
and challenge each other's
sense of danger and humor

**beautiful heroic catalina
yet another gift**

raw meat and candles
knowing how to make the best out of the worst
in mexican paradise

lit candles
on a pelican skeleton
while sucking in
the mexican marijuana

full of self protection
and early private bedtime

# Catalina

# Yoga years

i woke up in our apartment
317 west 93 street
my wife and our children
so very hung over
bad hung over

our children there
in my 30's

it hit me hard
that was enough
the booze
the smokes
the slow suicide

I walked down
broadway
to 73rd street
the satchidananda
yoga institute

gave myself to it

"you are not your body
 you are not your mind"

easy to stop everything
they made it so clear
the ego is bullshit

    did the all of it

gave up all the crap
booze smokes meat
and the rest
it worked

body good mind clear

everything going good

got a gig with a famous band
good money treated well
doing yoga every day
in comfortable hotels

playing to huge crowds
brought an electric pot
on the road
to cook my brown rice
and buckwheat

after months with the band

on a flight
the flight attendant
asked if anyone wanted
a drink

I ordered a double martini
and a pack of pall malls
no reason
that was the beginning
of the end

we were in a motel
in florida

STEPHEN JAY GOLDBERG

all the guys in the band
came into my room
sweet good talented guys

they simply said
"steve can you not
drink before the gigs"
which were big concerts

I was shocked
had no idea
thought I was
playing great

that night
I didn't drink
the saxophone player
said in my ear
nice to have you
back on the bandstand

I had no idea

I didn't like the
saxophone player
yet got him the gig
he was good
but a show off

I roomed with him
waking up to
the scent of pot
every morning

he would say
stevie what are
we doing here

no one calls me
stevie

years later
I heard he killed himself

he played okay
but a pain in the ass

should have never
gotten him
into the band

won't name him
r.g. I guess
you became
a pain in the ass
to yourself

so, so, so
sitting in the plaza
at night
everyone drunk or high on something
not me
I'm dizzy and not Gillespie

MAYBE THE LACK OF BOOZE
THE LACK OF SMOKING
OR JUST BEING SO TIRED
OR TOO MUCH BLASTING SUN
I CAN'T SLEEP
NEED, NEED, NEED
TO BE AROUND PEOPLE

tonight I feel like I'm going to
at last die
get this shit over with

MAYBE IT'S PLAYING THE TRUMPET
SO HARD
NIGHT AFTER NIGHT AFTER NIGHT
THE PRESSURE ON THE BRAIN AND LIPS

the interesting thing about alcohol is
it removes fear
then sends postcards back in the morning

THE FEAR AND TREMBLING BACK TENFOLD
SO IT REQUIRES MORE ALCOHOL
TO REMOVE THE FEAR AND TREMBLING AND LONELINESS
I LOVE THAT
THE FUCKING CYCLE OF TRUTH
THE ILLUSION OF FEAR AND TREMBLING AND TRUTH
AND YES FREEDOM

so it's confusing, so what
so is Beethoven and Bach and Charlie Parker
confusing if you try to analyze

OUR BIG FAT BRAINS
SO MUCH TROUBLE
WE HAVE TO SHUT THEM UP
THE ENDLESS CHATTER AND BABBLE
SHUT UP
TURN DOWN THE VOLUME

everyone out here chattering
in Spanish and English
and attempt at communication
the never ending search
for love and sex and affection

I'M SO SOBER I'M REALLY SPINNING
LIKE I'VE BEEN ON A SAILBOAT
TRYING TO GET MY LAND LEGS BACK

I don't want to pass out
here on the street
funny that people
would think I'm drunk

I'LL TRY TO WALK BACK AND NOT FALL
DRINK A LOT OF WATER
HERE GOES...

so I made it
having a cup of water
with vodka and mango juice
and a smoke

I JUST WANT A WOMAN
TO RUB MY BACK
AND TELL ME IT'S OKAY
WHICH IT'S NOT

STEPHEN JAY GOLDBERG

# CONFESSIONS

i don't like confessions or secrets
there's a saying in AA
you're only as sick as your secrets
see there's a confession
i've been to AA

i loved it
except for the part
about not drinking
the whole concept of AA
is beautiful

the 12 steps
the 12 traditions
the 12 chromatic notes
the 12 months
blah, blah, blah
fill it in

we jews don't have confession
but we do have our day of atonement
to be forgiven for our sins
i never did it
i don't want to be forgiven

i want to be punished

i want to be punished
by a woman in a tight transparent white silk bra
snake-skin high-heeled boots
and a spider-webbed thong that exposes
delicate black hair on her inner thighs

i want her to be a high priestess
a rabbi, a buddha, a goddess
who makes me cry and beg
who clears up all the shit
all the lies and ego crap
a goddess who bathes me in her
warm enlightened lotus piss

a masked buddha-woman
with a voice like 12 grain sand paper
who inhales long thin cuban cigars
and wears false eyelashes
and black mascara
and has fucked a million men
and has sucked a million women

i want her to tell me
how ugly i am
how stupid i am
and how my life
has been a
more than terrible waste of time

i want her
to put her high-heeled
snake-skinned boot
into my mouth
so hard that it breaks my teeth

then down my throat
so my bullshit lies choke me
and my ego makes me vomit
out words and blood and dreams and hopes
that will never come true

then her left snake-skinned boot
up my ass
the terrible pain erases thought
erases hope and ambition

all that's left is sexuality
looking up at her thighs
the hair sneaking out
through the damp-stained thong

then she does it
with an old-style man's
silver glistening sharp shaving razor

she cuts it all away
balls, prick, prostate
a nice clean blood filled slice
her snake heel going deeper

all I know is i want her
i love her
i need her
i believe in her
she is the goddess

i want her so very bad
i want to give her the one-millionth and one orgasm
the one she's never had
the one i owe her
for truth
but she's cut it all away

she moves away
sitting in the leather chair
opening her legs
taking the parts
she has cut from me

ripping the thong aside
exposing the innocent wet opening
my dying eyes still able to focus
warm blood running down my thighs

she pushes my very
still hard body parts
inside her
wetness

i can hardly focus
she makes a sound
that sounds
like joy and pain

her thighs drip
the black leather chair
is soaked with blood
as she twists
and breathes so hard

my last vision
her wide open nostrils
my ego gone
severed forever

the sound of her breathing
slowly decrescendos
till i'm finally
in the nothing
i've waited for

i mean is that too much to ask for

# Counterpoint

it's late

time runs down his chin
a drooling
unshaven man
who doesn't know
he's in stroke mode
in a hospital bed

his medication
sleeps
on the wired bedside

he doesn't know
that he doesn't know

the blessings are the dreams
awake dreams

in a speeding red sports car
through the narrow streets of paris
his hand on the swollen gearshift
eyes through the cracked windshield

the woman
there is always a woman
reciting french poetry

his right hand slides from the gearshift
to her wet thighs
the music is screaming
high note fast jazz trumpets

the old man feels so young
and handsome
so filled with power
unaware of the catheter in his prick
or the childish doctors
watching the machine of his heartbeat

the red sports car
speeds to the open french countryside
hit by the
full pocked marked white moon

the young doctor's watch
the heartbeat slowing down

he sees the speedometer
at 90, at 100, 120
he pumps the gas
150

her long hair flying in the speed
of the wind
of the stars and moon
200 miles an hour

she brings her face
next to him
an open kiss on the mouth
her eyes close
his eyes close

she whispers something in french

yet another gear
the speed unknown
too fast to measure
in the speeding red
top down sports car

**224**

the young doctors
decide not to do the paddles
of revival
he's gone
as the beautiful young french woman
gives him a blinding
goodbye kiss

they choose
who will tell the
waiting family

they themselves children
who can't explain
the beautiful smile
on the old man's
dead face

the children cry
as they should,
in honor and grief

# Mexican hangover

**This is bad, really bad**
The worst hangover ever
Really memorable

Interesting because Mexico has been
A hangover free zone
It must be in the air

**Why, why, why**
**Do I do this to myself**
Head splitting
All shaky and spinning
As the palm trees
Dance in the warm breeze

My brain feels like
a deflated inner tube
In black squid ink

Yet I can't say, never again
Unless this kills me

**Did anyone ever die from a hangover**
I think so

Last night I made new friends
A 28 year old beautiful female doctor
And her sister, a singer

I had played the trumpet
With so much power and freedom

Then this young couple from Boulder
Came over
We sat by the pool
And talked for hours
We hugged
They said, I have to come and visit
And stay with them
All of the love and goodness

I don't remember their names
They drank endless beers
I drank a liter of vodka
Smoked three packs of Delicado cigarettes
They smoked too

I knew I was over my limit
But it was all so good
No, no sex
Sex would've been impossible
A bad messy idea

**As it always waits in it's dark corner**

Waking up I realize
I have an estranged niece in Boulder
Marla, my brother's first daughter

Poor Jay dead at 37
Cancer, cancer, cancer
The evil demon that doesn't want me yet
You fucker
Too late to get me young, you fucker

And I complain about
A self-inflicted hangover
Fuck, I should be nailed to the cross
Like a good Jew

How can I write this
I don't know
I can't move off this
Comfortable pool lounge chair
Maybe another dive in the pool
Poor me, poor me
Boo-hoo, boo-hoo
Poor Stephen

**So yeah, cheer up**
**Life is beautiful**
**Blue Mexican sky**
**Hot burning sun**
**The Pacific ocean so vast**
**The bird songs and their magical flights**

# No RIM SHOTS

I'M TIRED OF BEING
FUNNY AND CLEVER
IT COMES EASY
BUT IT'S REALLY
ALL FUCKIN DARK

SO GIVE ME A BREAK
OKAY, OKAY
I NEED TO NOT FUCK AROUND
WITHOUT THE RIM SHOTS
AND LAUGH TRACKS

SOMETIMES ONE HAS TO
GIVE UP WHAT THEY'RE
GOOD AT
AND NAIL THE TRUTH
WITH A SLEDGEHAMMER

SOMETIMES
WE HAVE TO GIVE UP
WHAT WE LOVE
TO MAKE ROOM
IN THE BOTTOM DRAWER
FOR SOME NEW UNKNOWN
UNDERWEAR

A STORY
TOLD BY A MEMBER
OF MILES DAVIS'
NEW EXPERIMENTAL BAND

MILES WAS FEELING SICK
HE ASKED THE BAND
TO PLAY A BALLAD
THEY DIDN'T KNOW HOW
SO HIS PIANO PLAYER
PROMPTED THEM

NEEDLESS TO SAY
IT WAS BEAUTIFUL
AND TENDER

AFTER THE SET
THE PIANO PLAYER
ASKED MILES
WHY HE DOESN'T
PLAY BALLADS ANYMORE

MILES SAID
BECAUSE I LOVE BALLADS
SO MUCH

THE SIGN OF A TRUE ARTIST

TO GIVE UP
WHAT YOU KNOW WORKS
AND TAKE CHANCES

MOST OF US
DON'T GIVE UP
WHAT WE LOVE
UNTIL
WHAT WE LOVE
GIVES US UP

THAT INCLUDES ME
I DON'T KNOW ABOUT YOU
AND YOUR
ILLUSION OF LONELINESS

AS MUCH AS I'D LIKE TO
FEEL WE'RE ALL PART OF EACH OTHER
AND PART OF THE BIG DEAL
IT MOST OFTEN DOESN'T FEEL LIKE THAT

IT FEELS LIKE WE'RE ALL
LOCKED IN OUR OWN BAG OF SKIN
THAT'S WHAT ALAN WATTS
CALLED IT, BAG OF SKIN

CERTAINLY FUCKING, LOVEMAKING
COMING
CHILD-MAKING
PHYSICAL CONTACT
MAKES IT FEEL BETTER

CREATING A NEW BAG OF SKIN
THAT WE FEED
AND LATER
GIVE THE CAR KEYS TO
AND WORRY THAT
IT DOESN'T CRASH
IN A MASS OF BENT STEEL

DEATH PATIENTLY WAITS
LIKE AN ABSCESSED TOOTH
IN A SLICK DENTIST'S OFFICE
WITH ALL THE LATEST MAGAZINES
WITH PHOTOS OF THE LATEST WAR
AND HALF NAKED MOVIE STARS

IN THE LAST MINUTES
OF A DEAN MARTIN ROAST
DEAN SAYS,
WE HAVE TO SAY GOODNIGHT

DON RICKLES ASKS,
ARE WE OUT OF JOKES?
DEAN SAYS
NO, OUT OF BOOZE

THE OTHER AFTERNOON
LAYING ON A SWING-BENCH
AT WATERFRONT PARK
LOOKING UP AT A TREE
LEAVES SWINGING IN THE BREEZE

IT HIT ME
ME AND THAT TREE
WE'RE MORE THE SAME
THAN DIFFERENT
SAME FOR THE CLOUDS
AND LAKE AND THE AIR
GOING THROUGH MY LUNGS

NOT SO SURE ABOUT
THE PEOPLE ORDERING
THEIR DOGS AROUND
AND PICKING UP DOG SHIT
IN LITTLE PLASTIC BAGS

I MEAN
WHO LOVES WHO
AND HOW FAR DOES IT GO

BAGS OF SKIN
PLASTIC BAGS OF DOG SHIT
LATEX BAGS OF DYING COME
DESPERATE PHONE CALLS
OF SUICIDE

OUT OF JOKES DEAN
NO, OUT OF BOOZE

# Vacation

sometimes it's nice
not to care about

getting fat
**getting drunk**
smoking too much
**wasting time**
wasting money
**being in or out of love**
getting sick
**getting lost**
getting old
**being stupid**
dying

it's not advertised in the new york times
**vacation** section

# NOT Knowing

I don't know how
to play this game

this walking
between the tears
in and out of silent rooms
not knowing why I'm here

seeing all this beauty
so alone

the wind blowing
the leaves
that will soon fall

when do I
get to fall
and be blown away

"I write out of necessity,
NOT TO GO NUTS.

When everything's good,
I don't feel the need to write."

STEPHEN GOLDBERG IS A PLAYWRIGHT,
POET, JAZZ MUSICIAN.
ORIGINALLY FROM NEW YORK CITY, HE HAS LIVED
IN VERMONT FOR THE LAST 38 YEARS.
HE HAS WRITTEN AND DIRECTED OVER 26 PLAYS.

HIS LAST PUBLICATION SCREWED FIVE PLAYS
STEPHEN GOLDBERG, FOMITE PRESS.

WEBSITE: STEPHENJGOLDBERG.COM

Made in the USA
Middletown, DE
08 October 2023

40185305R00146